FOUR MINUS THREE

A Mother's Story

FOUR MINUS THREE

A Mother's Story

GUITELLE H. SANDMAN

2007

Cover design by Guitelle Sandman and Roger Gordy.
Book design by Roger Gordy.

To order additional copies, please contact us.
BookSurge, LLC
www.booksurge.com
1-866-308-6235
orders@booksurge.com

To Bob

TABLE OF CONTENTS

Birth is a beginning
And death a destination.
And life is a journey,
A sacred pilgrimage—
                    To life everlasting[1]

[1] *Gates of Repentance, Then New Union Prayerbook for the Days of Awe*, Central Conference of America Rabbis, 5738 New York 1978, (pp. 283-284).

FOREWORD

M ANY marriages end when a child dies. Although each of our three sons died in separate times and from different causes, my husband Bob and I have been married for fifty-six years. How did we survive such terrible losses? And what's kept us together? We've often wondered ourselves. Certainly we have not had a "story-book romance" and we've weathered many storms.

When we were twenty-one and twenty-three, with the blessing of my father and Bob's parents, we were married, but I'm sure had little understanding of what marriage was all about. In our favor was the fact that we'd both led sheltered, stable lives with intact families.

When we were hit with our tragedies we were fortunate to have emotional support from friends and extended family but we felt so raw and depressed we knew we needed more help. As a social worker, I knew the value of psychotherapy. I'd had lots of experience with death and in fact had helped others grieve. But this was different. This was very personal; this was happening to us. With each death it became apparent that both Bob and I needed therapy, which we used. This kind of support alleviated much of our pain and we were grateful for it. Still, I was haunted by many unanswered or even unanswerable questions. What happened to our dreams for our children? How could our family be so decimated? What makes life worth living when we have lost so much? Should I share our story?

I have always liked to write and often used writing as a way to get at my feelings – to express anger, frustration, and disappointment, even joy. I often join writers' groups. I think writers are interesting people and I enjoy listening to their stories and observing how they are written. However, I never find it easy to write in a group – I have to ponder what I want to say and do not like the pressure of having to produce something on the spot. One Saturday, however, I participated in a workshop at the Cambridge Center for Adult Education on the Use of Therapeutic Writing. I was curious about the topic and thought it might be useful to me.

In the crowded classroom we were given a visualization exercise. I knew this was going to be something I would not like. I don't exactly remember the assignment, but it was something like:

> Picture yourself in a special place where you happen to
> meet someone from your past. See what memories that
> chance meeting might evoke and write about the experience.

Since I was looking for a program where the teacher would lecture on the topic, I was not happy with an assignment that required me to produce. I felt trapped. Everyone else immediately began scribbling their stories. Pens were flying, papers turned. I sat there feeling inadequate. Close to the end of the writing time, a thought occurred to me and in fact, I had a vision and began to write:

> "It was a free and beautiful autumn day – crisp, clear, a
> bit nippy. I had no commitments, nothing I had to do, so
> it was a perfect day for a walk around the local lake where
> I knew there would be few people. I donned my parka, a
> scarf, some gloves, my walking shoes and off I went.
>
> At first I turned off my thinking apparatus and just
> sauntered along. Soon however, I began to notice the col-
> orful clusters of dried leaves on the ground, the signs of a
> changing, new season. Up ahead there was a batch of
> maple trees that were particularly brilliant. Among the
> leaves, I thought I saw a person but could not be sure.
> Shortly however, I saw a young man with coppery hair
> and thought of our two younger boys, who were both red
> heads. A body – a long, lanky body – emerged. I won-
> dered if that could be Jon. No, it couldn't – Jon has been
> gone over twenty years. But it looked like the way he
> walked. The person turned and peered at me. Goodness, it
> looked like Jon's freckled face, his big brown eyes. It
> looked like his grin. He was wearing blue jeans, a sweater
> and a windbreaker. It was Jon. He came closer as I stood
> stunned.
>
> 'Hi Mom,' he said, like he'd just been out for a walk
> and nothing had happened. I reached out to hug him,

but he was elusive. There seemed to be no substance, yet he was there.

'Jonny, can this be you? I want to hug you, touch you, feel you again.'

'I wish you could too, Mom, but that can't happen. I'm O.K. and I'm glad to see you here. You look older.'

'I am, Jonny, but you'll never be older. You look the same as the day I last saw you alive. I guess that's what happens when people die. They stay the same age forever in our hearts.'

'Mom, I have so many questions. I want to know how everyone is. What are they doing? I want to know what I've missed. I had so many dreams of what I might become, of having a family, or maybe being an anthropologist. Maybe you can help me. What are my friends doing? Do they have children? What kind of careers do they have? Does anyone miss me? Maybe you can finish my story.'

'Oh Jonny – I wish I could finish your story. Everyone misses you. I wish you were here with us now. We had such high hopes for you and you gave us much joy. We miss you and think of you every day. But I'm afraid we've been focusing on our own sadness and not enough about all the unfinished aspects of your life. We dream about what you might have done, what your life would have been like if you had lived, and of course, if you would have had children.'

Our conversation felt real to me, yet Jon was beginning to fade. We had so many questions for each other. Jon turned away and looked wistfully over his shoulder. 'I wish I could hug you, too, Mom.' He waved, smiled and disappeared, his coppery hair fading into the leaves. I stood filled with longing and sadness as I thought about his questions. Meeting him broke my sense of peace and left me empty, tantalized and heartbroken. It was no longer a sunny day for me."

I had not consciously thought of Jonny, our middle son, for a long time. It was an epiphany. I had never before been moved by a visualization exercise. The experience left me quite shaken.

In the course of my latest therapy, my therapist had suggested that I get a writing coach to help me put some of my thoughts together. But where could I find someone who did this? At lunch after the workshop, I got up my courage and spoke with Dr. Allan Hunter, the group's facilitator. I told him of the experience I had in his class and also mentioned that we had had many losses. I asked if he knew of a writing coach. "If you would like, I could work with you," he said, "and if that doesn't work out I'll try to find you someone else." I was elated. He had brought out something special in me and I trusted him. Thus this project and my journey of reflection and a different kind of grief work began.

Actually, writing this was not what I expected. Allan had me write about all kinds of memories and experiences going back to my childhood. I wrote about my ways of coping and each of the children's lives from their very beginning to their deaths. Of course, I wrote about our daughter too. When I worried that no one would want to or even should read some of the things I wrote, he assured me no one had to – it was simply a way to gain some insight and understanding, to put things in perspective. So with his guidance, I began.

Probably before we go on, I should describe our family. Bob and I were married young (I was still in college) but we both wanted a large family. I was an only child and Bob had only one sister. We waited until I graduated and then were eager to start having babies, which we did in rapid succession. By our eighth wedding anniversary we had four children, Mark, Martha, Jonathan and Roger. In fact, Roger was born on our eighth anniversary. Although I had been pre-med in college, I decided that it meant more to me to have a family than to struggle to go to medical school. Bob, an engineer, had a good, secure job in the family business and money did not seem to be a problem. Therefore, for twelve years after we were married, I stayed at home and did volunteer work. I managed a very busy household and loved it. Still, nagging at me was the idea that I should be somebody in my own right, that I should have a profession. Because medicine had always interested me, I decided that a career in medical social work was a logical choice. When Mark was ten and Roger four, I began my work on my MSW. Since I did this part time, it took me six years to complete my degree. That's what I did in the 1950's and 1960's, and despite the normal chaos of a busy family, they were happy years.

The 1970's were more tumultuous. Actually, they were difficult times. The Viet Nam War was disturbing and kids in their late teens and early twenties were rebelling in ways no one expected. Suddenly our contained, prosaic family had to deal with new and difficult issues, as did many others of that era.

Many have had worse tragedies than ours. I can't help but think of the Kennedy family who had tragedy after tragedy. This was particularly poignant to me because John. F. Kennedy, Jr. crashed his plane and died only a few weeks after Mark. Mark was not so handsome and certainly not so privileged, but they both had long faces and curly hair. I remember being glued to the television after JFK, Jr's tragic death, feeling for his family and marveling at the unfortunate endings for these two young men.

* * *

Many others have had multiple losses even worse then ours. There have been global disasters such as the terrible tsunami upheavals, wars, genocides, earthquakes, floods, and the Holocaust, where whole families have been eradicated. Such situations are unfathomable to me. All I can speak about is our own family with repeated deaths of young men who were deprived of fulfilling the promise of their lives. Our story is about how these events impacted their siblings and us and how we have struggled to find meaning in our lives and move on.

Mark was our third son to die; after that I felt a need to validate each of their lives, to let others know some of their background, struggles and successes. I wanted to give snapshots of our boys' early years, their individual development and family events.

What follows are my recollections, my perceptions, my memories of our family and our struggles, as we reacted to these personal tragedies. It is a mother's story, my story, told from my point of view. I'm sure some of my memories are distorted and not fully accurate or in the right time or order, but they are what I remember. The boys' lives as remembered by others are part of their legacy. I want to tell about our quite ordinary family that now feels tarnished, clouded.

Since Roger was the last-born, but the first to die, I'll begin with his story.

The others will follow.

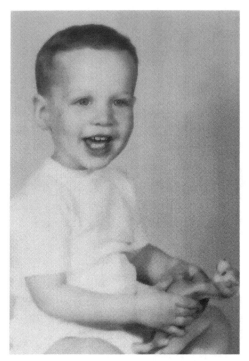

Mark April, 1954

Mark and Martha May 1955

Mark, Martha and Jonny November 1957

Mark, Martha, Jonny and Roger November 1959

Our Youngest Son, Roger

———— ❧ ————

ROGER, our youngest and the child with the most needs, was born on our eighth wedding anniversary, which we thought was a good omen. He was the only baby we had by appointment, the only one who took a long time to be born, and the only one who from the beginning had a difficult life because of his numerous handicaps. He was a sweet, sensitive little boy who struggled to be "like everyone else". Perhaps that was his greatest wish. However, he wasn't. He was his own special person. We tried to give him every opportunity we could; we failed at many but we did the best we could to enable him to have a satisfactory life.

In retrospect we probably put too much pressure on him. We wanted him to succeed; we wanted him to be happy; we wanted him to feel good about himself. We were aware of his difficulties and ached for him. I suppose, looking back, that we were hard on him although that was not our intent. We just wanted to enable him to make the most of his abilities, as we did with each of our children.

His life began in this way on September 3, 1958. Since Jonny was born shortly after I arrived at the hospital, my doctor thought it would be more prudent for me to be induced this time. Therefore, although I got to the hospital early in the morning, the baby was not born until late afternoon. And in spite of being induced, I still had a natural delivery without drugs.

The doctor was concerned because it was a dry birth (very little amniotic fluid) but he thought the delivery went well and the baby was fine. I was so relieved to have the birth over with, and the baby safely delivered that I did not worry about any complications. I was euphoric and tired.

What a surprise to see I had another boy and that he was lovely, robust, with all his fingers and toes! He weighed 7 lbs. 10 oz., had bright red hair and seemed quite placid. The nursery nurses joked and said he looked like Tom Sawyer. We named him Roger Eliot after his great-grandfather who had just died. Actually, we thought he was going to be Elizabeth. I don't know why we, or I, thought he was going to be a girl. At any rate, we were glad to have him even though we had to scramble around for a name again.

Now we had four children and Mark, the oldest, was not quite six. Roger entered a very busy household and was not particularly welcomed by the others. Mark thought we had enough redheads in the family so was not enchanted to have another.

Martha said, "I don't want any more brothers. I want a baby sister," and she hardly talked to us for a few days. Jonny at two and a half was curious about the new arrival, but didn't say anything. It was not a great reception for this new baby.

I, however, was delighted to have another infant. By now I was an experienced Mom, enjoying the closeness that comes with nursing. Of course I could have done without the older kids bringing their friends over to watch. Roger was indeed a calm, affectionate little baby but seemed slower to do things than I thought was normal.

When I asked our pediatrician about this he said, "All the others were very active and fast. Roger is fine. He's just different. Relax and enjoy him." Still, we worried about him. He was alert and responsive and made little talking noises but he rolled over late, sat up late, crawled late dragging one leg behind him and walked and talked late. Even after he was walking, he had an awkward gait.

The older children expressed some concern. "Why isn't Roger like Susie's brother? Why isn't he walking yet? Why can't he talk like Bobby's brother?" We answered that every baby develops at his own rate and that Roger would catch up. Nevertheless, we were troubled too.

When Roger began talking, he had a lot to say but his speech was unintelligible. We got used to the way he spoke and his friends on the street seemed to understand him but most people, including his grandparents, could not. We took him to Parmenter Health Center where children with speech difficulties were evaluated. Their report said he would outgrow his problems but in fact his speech remained "slushy" and he could not make the sounds of "l", "s" and "m" as well as others. He wore "docks and dues" on his feet and his sister was "Narfa". But he got along.

When he started nursery school he was friendly, outgoing and eager to go. He participated in all the activities. At age four, however, he was jumping up and down in his socks on the kitchen floor between Bob and me when he fell. We picked him up and tried to comfort him but to no avail, so we decided he was tired and carried him up to bed for a nap. After a while, we checked on him but he was still whimpering. "My leg hurts too much to stand; I can't walk," he said.

At first, we thought he was exaggerating but then decided we should check. We took him to the emergency room at the Newton-Wellesley Hospital where an X-ray revealed a broken tibia. He had a full leg cast applied and was given crutches. We blamed ourselves for not recognizing his problem, but he didn't seem to care and enjoyed the attention he got.

* * *

Once at home, he never had the coordination to manage the crutches so he hitched himself around on his bottom. Because he was no longer upright he had to miss school. Soon we got a call from his teacher. "Could you please bring Roger in so the children can see him? The kids think his leg has broken off, and they'd be reassured to see that it's still attached." We did and Roger was as glad to see his friends, as they were to see him. However, he was so hard on his cast that it had to be patched several times before he had it removed. Once the cast was off, he quickly recovered and soon was running around again.

In kindergarten Roger settled in but seemed socially behind the other children. His speech continued to be poor and his movements were awkward. Finally we took him to a pediatric neurologist who said Roger had cerebral palsy, a condition usually caused by a birth injury or brain lesion. Since Roger's birth was apparently normal, although fairly dry, no one had worried about a problem. I did not blame anyone. Actually I was relieved to have a diagnosis, since previously I felt I was the only one concerned about his development.

While the CP, except for Roger's awkwardness, was not obvious, the doctor predicted he would have difficulty with certain small motor activities. He said Roger would probably be able to ride a bike and ski, but not skate. Writing would be hard for him and there would be learning difficulties. He suggested we have a psychologist evaluate him.

At that time, we told our parents about Roger's diagnosis but were met with denial. My father announced that it was not so. It was unlike him to be unwilling to accept such news and one of the few times I wanted his support and did not get it. Bob's parents dismissed this information also, as if we were making it up. None of our parents knew or wanted to know what this diagnosis entailed. It made me feel that in some way Roger's problem was a disgrace, something to be hidden, and that, in a way, we were at fault. I was hurt by the reaction of all three of our parents.

Ironically, I had been volunteering at a school for children with cerebral palsy so I made arrangements for their psychologist to test him. We went to her office in Cambridge. I stayed outside and listened while they were working together.

"Could you draw me a square?" I heard.

"No"

"Well how about a circle?"

"No"

"Well, I am going to draw a square"

"That's silly," Roger replied, "That's not a square, that's a circle – I'll show you a square."

And so the test continued. The report was that he was an intelligent little boy but that he would learn differently from others. She thought it would be a good idea to begin each school year by talking to his teachers.

Thus began Roger's education. Each year I talked with his teachers. Some were interested but couldn't believe Roger might have problems. After all, his brother Jon was such a good student. We discussed the difference between the boys and that Roger had difficulty articulating his words, developing his small muscle coordination and often understanding how to relate to the other kids. Since Roger was among the younger children in his class and would likely have more challenges in school because he was poorly coordinated, we persuaded his elementary school principal to keep him in kindergarten another year to give him a better foundation, which turned out to be a good move. At the time Roger did not seem to mind. He became more self-confident.

By the time he was in first grade, he clearly was ready. For one thing, he had friends, since several children on our street were also in his grade. In fact, in first grade Roger did very well. He was a quick, omnivorous, retentive reader – an asset that gave him some status. Socially he still had some problems since his movements were clumsy and slow. If he had to tie his shoes or put on boots, he had trouble keeping up with the others and often needed extra help. His speech was unclear and other children complained about not understanding him or else ridiculed him. Fortunately the Newton school system had good speech therapists. Roger had started speech therapy in kindergarten and we paid privately to continue it over the summer. His speech became clearer although he still had difficulty with a few sounds. He spent many hours practicing, which included licking peanut butter from the roof of his mouth and chewing bubble gum. He was a good sport and cooperative but progress was very slow.

While I was glad to have professional help, much of the responsibility for overseeing Roger's practice and exercise fell on me. It was a chore for both of us when we would each rather have being doing something else. And always in the back of my mind I wondered how long he would need special attention and what else we might have to deal with in the future.

We did not tell Roger that he had CP until he was eight. Since his disability was relatively mild, especially in comparison with CP children I had worked with, I hoped that if we just gave him enough encouragement and support he could do anything. We did not want him to use his diagnosis as a way out of trying. This was wrong. Roger actually was as relieved as I was to learn that some of the reasons he was different from his friends was because of CP. Knowing this enabled him to feel better about himself; his problems were not his fault and he tried to be like everyone else.

By the fifth grade it was clear that Roger had real learning difficulties. We had him tested at Children's Hospital where it was determined that he had problems in math and in writing. He easily took in information but had a great deal of trouble processing it and putting it on paper. We asked the school for special help or tutoring but the principal said they had limited resources and that Roger read very well. Because reading was the most important skill to be learned in elementary school, they had specialists for dyslexia but, at that time, they had no resources to help him with his dysgraphia and dyscalculia.

We were frantic and hated to see our child floundering. In sixth grade, we enrolled him at the Carroll School for children with learning difficulties. At first, it seemed like a good move. Roger began to be successful in small classes and to enjoy new subjects like Latin. Unfortunately, the school only went through seventh grade. His teachers thought Proctor Academy in Andover, N.H. would be a good place for him to go next, since they were supposed to have special programs

5

for children with learning difficulties.

This was a wrench for all of us. Expensive boarding school was not in our plans. Furthermore, we liked having him at home. To send him away made me feel like a bad parent. Also, I was concerned about his skipping eighth grade because Proctor started in the ninth. The Carroll School determined that Roger could handle the transition since he was advanced in several areas. We discussed the idea with Roger who said he would be glad to be in ninth grade. "It'll be an adventure, Mom. I'll be O.K." So off he went leaving us feeling guilty, sad, and certainly apprehensive. Fortunately, although he was young and vulnerable, he was also spunky and that helped both him and us.

At first, all went well. He was happy, seemed to get along with the other boys, and enjoyed the skiing and most of his classes. His second year, however, was a disaster. He simply did not do his work or turn in his papers. The teachers and his advisor at school tried to put pressure on him and to motivate him but nothing seemed to work. He was doing very poorly, especially in algebra. We called the school. "Do you think a tutor would help? We'd be glad to pay for one." We were told that he did not need a tutor, and that with some effort he could probably get a D. He had to learn to do his work and "toe the line". We were dismayed and furious, yet did not know where to turn. Even though we were not educators, we knew that it is damaging to anyone's self esteem and motivation to be told that you had to work extra hard to achieve minimal results.

He barely got through the year. One of his teachers told us that Roger read every book in the library except what was assigned. That passive aggression seemed to be Roger's way of skirting the issues. At any rate, when we approached Roger about coming home for high school and probably repeating tenth grade, which would put him back with his former classmates, he was agreeable. He really did not complain to us about his Proctor experience while he was there or later. My sense is that when there, he just withdrew into his books. At the time we did not know if he was badgered or ridiculed by the other boys; he just seemed to do his own thing. Still, I think he was relieved to be coming home and we were glad to have him back.

Once he returned to Newton Schools, he wrote several papers that described what he had been feeling but not talking about with us. For example, we came across one paper in which he wrote:

"I am afraid of physical activity. The reason for this is that I suffer from cerebral palsy but so little as to be unnoticeable by my peers but of which I am painfully aware. Every time I'm called on to play basketball, touch football, etc., I cringe. People seem to think that any tall person is a fantastic basketball player or that someone of large size is good in football, neither of which I excel at. Elementary sports were terrifying for me. I was invariably always picked last for any team. I couldn't hit a baseball or kick a football and soon was lowered to the status of a girl in the eyes of the best athletes, who did everything effortlessly. I did have some consolations. There were always one or two people who couldn't run very fast or climb ropes very well. My hopes were short lived, for these few always outdid me in hockey and football. The only time that I was able to feel really good about myself was during a lunch period game of bombardment. I, of everyone else on my team, stayed on the court, thus winning the round.

Summer camps for me were terrible – some had a system of grading each activity. I failed because my lack of eye hand coordination got in my way with everything I tried – the other campers seeing my inabilities would start jeering me, while the counselors retreated, leaving me to defend myself. As a result of this treatment, I was ashamed of myself.

In the summer of 1969, I went to Northwoods, a YMCA camp where my brothers had gone. Although the camp was athletically inclined, I got by, but the declaration by another camper, "You stink!" during a relay race, has stuck in my mind. In 1970 I went to a camp where luck was with me for it had a primary focus on the arts, which I could handle and I went back there, to Interlocken in New Hampshire, two summers more.

At Proctor Academy I was bombarded with team sports – in spring of my freshman year I participated in baseball, finding myself on the bench at almost every game – by spring of my sophomore year I chose lacrosse and finally found a sport that I could do well at –"

When Roger returned home, we had him reevaluated at Children's Hospital. This was followed by a conference at Newton South High School where we met with the principal, his guidance counselor and a few teachers. Again they referred to his older brother Jon and said it was hard to believe Roger could have these learning problems. Once this was clarified and documented with the help of our consulting psychologist, Dr. Irving Hurwitz, they agreed to work with us. We felt it was very useful to have a voice of authority come with us to validate Roger's needs. Otherwise, we had learned that parents tend to be regarded as complainers who want special attention for their child. We felt we needed this documentation of his test results and the recommendations of a professional to get appropriate attention and cooperation. Newton South did work with us and with the outside help we provided for Roger. As a result, Roger was very happy to be back in the main stream and seemed to fit in well

Dr. Hurwitz recommended a professor at MIT to work with Roger on math. Dr. Alan Natapoff was a scientist who was interested in children who could not learn math. He had devised a special program whereby he would work with the kids privately and then have them tutored by students from MIT and Harvard whom he had trained in his method. A parent had to attend each of the sessions with Dr. Natapoff in order to reinforce what was learned during the sessions. That meant me. Then I was required to work with him at home every night.

This created a crisis for our family. Because I had always felt mathematically challenged, I did not feel up to the task. I had hoped Bob, the engineer and mathematician, would go with Roger and then help with the homework at night. Unfortunately, Bob said he could not possibly take time off during the day. Because he was our chief breadwinner, I deferred to him but was angry. Furthermore, I resented having to adjust my schedule to accommodate Roger's needs while Bob did nothing to alter his. I felt I was doing all the parenting, teaching and adjusting. I still had a professional career, other children to care for, and a household to run and Bob was not sensitive to my stress. However, it was clear Roger needed help and we did what we could. In a family where there is a child with special needs, there is a ripple effect. That child gets the attention but everyone else pays a price.

Dr. Natapoff was a big, warm, teddy bear of a man who was positive, kindly and gentle, but persistent in his approach. I never heard him say,

"You're wrong," but rather, "I guess I didn't explain this well enough. Let's try it another way." Roger loved him and after each session had a big grin and seemed to grow another few inches. Every night we worked on math with little resistance from Roger. This was hard for me and I remember very little about the method. Bob went out most evenings to his political meetings and other civic endeavors while my evenings were spent working with Roger on math. We still had three other children at home and all my energy seemed to be going to Roger. I felt the other kids needed attention and longed for some time for myself.

Our work at MIT continued for about four months. After one session, Dr. Natapoff said, "Now you've done long division."

Roger answered, "I can't do long division. I've never been able to do long division."

"But you've done it. You really are doing long division!"

Roger could hardly believe his ears. He was ecstatic, and so was I. I began to see a more hopeful future.

At the beginning of his sophomore year, Roger was doing math at about the third grade level; by Christmas, he was doing grade level algebra and geometry (ordinary grade level, not advanced). We were all thrilled. After this, we had tutors several times a week for the next three years because Roger insisted on taking math but I was relieved of my burden of coaching. These young women from Harvard and MIT were extraordinary – bright, warm, patient, and giving. Part of Roger's success was that he enjoyed working with them and wanted to please them. They took the long subway ride from Cambridge to our house in Waban in all kinds of weather. We also credit the school for working with our plan. Roger continued in high school with his tutors at home but he took his exams like everyone else and felt good about his achievements. His SAT scores in math were acceptable and his English scores high. Roger was probably an overachiever.

However, again in a paper we recently retrieved, Roger continued to describe his experiences as he wrote:

"At Newton South, there was less pressure to join an athletic team. In spite of this, I had to face the school "jocks" who presumed I had great athletic prowess, probably due to my size, but their disdain for me did not die. The contempt they held for me was expressed rather vilely in my junior year when two members of the football team, passing me in the hall said, "What do you know, a faggot!" The words stung like a whip.

In the short span of my life, I have encountered many pitfalls in physical education activities and suffered much humiliation by my peers and on occasion by my instructors. The object of my trouble is entirely invisible, except to me, and if it were not for this aspect of my body, I would not always be afraid of physical activities relying on motor coordination."

Roger's life, as he himself noted, was not easy. As a baby and young child he was plagued with severe eczema needing to have his weeping, bleeding, itching skin bandaged. When all the children got mumps, he not only had mumps, but also mumps encephalitis.

"Can you move your head, Rog?"

"No."

What a scare that was for us! He just lay in bed with a very high fever and a distant bewildered expression. He hardly complained or fussed, but must have been miserable. Fortunately the encephalitis was viral and after about a week, much to our relief, he recovered.

The summer Roger was three years old the family took off on one of our camping trips. This time it was through upstate New York. The station wagon was loaded with all our gear, tents, sleeping bags, duffle bags and, of course the six of us. As he was closing the station wagon for the final time, Bob did not realize Roger was standing there with his finger in the door. Unfortunately, there was a deep wound, so our first stop was the Newton-Wellesley Hospital where a resident cleaned and stitched Roger's finger.

"We're planning a camping trip, do you think it is O.K. for him to go?" we asked the doctor.

He replied, "Oh sure, just keep the finger clean and dry." Since we were all set, we decided to proceed.

Along the way, I said, "I don't feel comfortable with this. I think we should call our own doctor."

"O.K., when we stop for lunch."

We did and the doctor said Roger's shots were probably up to date but he'd recommend a tetanus booster. So our next stop was to find a hospital, which we did in Oneonta, NY.

We had planned to cover a lot of ground on this trip and therefore we did not stay in one place very long. But we spent almost every morning wringing and drying out and going to Laundromats because the season was so wet. We also had a new tent that we thought was waterproof. One morning we awoke to find that Roger had edged his way out of his sleeping bag and off the air mattress. He was blissfully sleeping with his face in a puddle of water. So much for keeping his finger dry! When we camped at Buttermilk Falls near Ithaca, all the others were sliding down the falls, happily screeching and laughing. Poor Roger had to enjoy the water as much as he could with his hand held high by his mother. As usual, he was a good sport but it was a disappointment to him and me. I think everyone thought it was just Mom's job to take care of others. However, whenever I saw the scar on his finger thereafter, I felt pangs of guilt that we had done this to him and just added to his troubles.

Soon after Roger got his driver's license, he was riding in the back seat with Bob and me when we heard a strange noise from the rear. I asked, "What's going on Rog?" and heard only a grunt or groan and looked behind. There was Roger having a seizure. We were terrified and actually did not know exactly what it was. It probably did not last more than a few minutes. We stopped the car and I climbed in the back seat and held him. When the seizure was over he was a bit dazed but did not seem flustered. We did not know what to make of this. When we all felt calmer, I returned to the front seat and we went home. No one talked.

I called our doctor who referred us to a neurologist at Children's Hospital. Roger told him he had had other episodes in his room, "I thought I saw clowns and bright lights and then I blanked out. I didn't worry too much about it and didn't tell anyone." The doctor said this was an aura and that it was a good way to predict a seizure. He ordered an electroencephalogram and then confirmed that Roger did indeed have a seizure disorder (he urged us not to call it epilepsy because of the stigma of that diagnosis). He prescribed Dilantin as well as a full in-patient work-up. He also said that Roger could not drive until he was free of seizures for at least six months. While Roger understood, it was quite a blow. Getting his license had been a great achievement for him and an important rite of passage.

Roger went for his work-up willingly and seemed relieved to learn that there was an official diagnosis for his problem, just as he had been relieved when he learned that he had CP. There proved to be no further seizures but the Dilantin caused hyperplagia in his gums necessitating regular visits to the periodontist. The doctor suggested another drug that would not affect his gums. He would need to have blood levels checked regularly. This made me nervous so I looked it up in the Physicians' Desk Reference, an encyclopedia of prescription drugs, and learned that one of the side effects could be aplastic anemia. I explained to Roger what changing the drug could entail and Roger decided he would rather be chained to the periodontist's chair for regular visits rather than take that risk. His neurologist was angry with me for questioning his recommendation and said he would prefer to see Roger alone from that time on. It was just one more thing for Roger and me to deal with.

Much to our chagrin, Roger did not hesitate to tell his friends that he had epilepsy. He seemed to feel that it made him special and freely talked to them about his seizure. They didn't quite know what to make of it but except for the driving it did not change his life. It was a bigger issue for me as I worried about the implications of this for his future. Would he ever be able to drive, to be fully independent? What if he had more seizures that were less discreet? How would he cope? How would we? It felt like we were never going to be "out of the woods" because he had many chronic problems and needed so much attention and supervision.

Despite these setbacks, Roger had some successes and fun in high school. He loved the theater and films. Whatever he saw, he not only knew the actors but also cited the director, producer and others involved in the production. Roger was no star but he was a participant. In the high school production of *Sweet Charity* he had many roles, each of which involved a change of costumes and about one line of dialogue. A non-singer, he also managed to be in the concert choir. At his high school awards night, he received a Theater Arts Award that pleased him, and us, enormously. He was so happy to be part of things.

He enjoyed language study, especially Spanish. Although he had been indifferent to Spanish at Proctor, he loved it at Newton South. He was so eager to learn to speak Spanish we decided he could go to Spain after his sophomore year. We found a program in Valencia where he would live with a family, speak Spanish with them and take an appropriate course at the University of Valencia. It turned out to be a most successful adventure. He wrote wonderful letters home, enjoyed his family in Valencia, felt comfortable and proud of his money management and became quite fluent in Spanish. He even received a certificate from the Institute of Spanish Studies, which he treasured.

On his return, Martha, Bob and I met him in New York. We watched him come through customs dressed in his khaki pants and his green sport jacket. He looked grown-up and confident and greeted us with a big grin and bear hug.

By the time Roger was a senior in high school, there were other issues. He was awkward and still had trouble making friends. He was interested in girls but did not know how to relate to them. Some made fun of him, some ignored him, but fortunately his friends in the neighborhood stood by him. For his senior prom he wanted desperately to have a date and go. He invited Maura Fitzgerald, a young lady in his class who must have been less than five feet tall. Roger was a husky six feet three inches. The Mutt and Jeff look did not seem to bother either of them and Roger tried to be very courtly with his date and felt special in his tuxedo.

The event became complicated when the issue of transportation arose. Fortunately one of his friends in the neighborhood, Don Mayer, invited Roger to go with him and it turned out to be a happy, successful evening.

We were not sure what the next step would be. Should he go to college? If so, should it be a junior or a four year college? School was so arduous for him we felt it would be torture for him as well as us. We suggested a junior college. Roger was indignant and adamant. "I want to go to a real college like everyone else. I'm not stupid. I can do it." We searched for an appropriate institution and came up with the Boston University School of Basic Studies, which had a two-year program. After his interview, Roger was eager to go. The school had many kids who needed extra or transitional help and was able to provide some of the supervision we felt he still needed. We were told that 85% of their students went on to get their bachelor's degree, either at BU or elsewhere. Furthermore, Roger would be in a regular dorm, which excited him. We also felt that the proximity to home would provide some security for all of us. It proved to be an excellent choice and Roger not only did average, satisfactory work but was happy there. He finished his freshman year and eagerly looked forward to the next year. We all anticipated more growth and academic success. We certainly did not expect what would unfold.

Roger 1965

Roger at Proctor

Roger and Jon 1973

15

The Unexpected Happens

⚘

THREE weeks into his sophomore year, we got a call from Roger. "Mom, we're having an ethnic party in our dorm. Can you bring some chopped liver and maybe a noodle pudding?"

"Sure, we'll bring them over Saturday morning."

"Also Mom, I'm not feeling very well. I have terrible cramps, and diarrhea and I'm nauseous."

"Gee, I'm sorry Rog. Try to drink as much fluid as you can. This will probably pass in a few days. I'm sorry you're sick before your party."

We went to his dorm Saturday morning and he did not look well. We encouraged him to drink and brought him some ginger ale and saltines. As we left, we just thought he had a stomach bug and did not worry.

On Monday, we called to see how he was feeling. "Not very good. I'm still very sick to my stomach and can't eat or drink. I didn't even go to the party." I became more concerned, but thought sometimes stomach problems can last a while.

"Perhaps you'd better go to the infirmary," I suggested.

On Tuesday, however, a call came from our pediatrician. "Roger's here in my office. He came in leaning on his roommate and he's quite sick. I think he may have hepatitis. At any rate, you'd better come to take him home. I'll send a lab to your house in the morning to do more blood work." As I drove to the doctor's office, I was still not too worried. When I picked him up, however, Roger looked terrible. His face was ghostly white so that his freckles gave him an eerie grayish appearance. He was dizzy and unbalanced. When he saw me, he seemed relieved. I helped him into the car.

He needed quite a bit of help getting from the car into the house. Once there, he plopped onto a kitchen chair and looked dazed.

"Do you want to lie down in your room?"

"No, I don't think I have enough strength to go upstairs. I just want to lie down."

"O.K., let's make up the bed in Grandpa's room."

It was a little bedroom off the kitchen. Thus began a long night. Roger became delirious, tried to get up, but staggered as he reached to hold onto the walls. He slept fitfully, talking and groaning in his sleep. When I came downstairs several times during the night, I found him sprawled on the floor or sitting on the edge of his bed. He was mumbling unintelligibly.

By seven in the morning, I called the doctor again and told him I was frightened. He said someone from the lab would come soon and then we should take him to Children's Hospital. He'd see us in the emergency room. Once the laboratory technician came, she commented that we had a very sick boy here, which was no news to us. Meanwhile, Roger was in and out of consciousness.

At one point he said, "Mom, I see myself in a half open coffin – and Grandpa's already dead!"

"Oh Roger, that's scary; you'll be all right," I said, hopefully trying to reassure him and myself as well. My father at that time was in a nursing home, very ill with cancer but still alive. He died the next week.

When the technician left, I told Bob that I could not manage Roger alone in the car and that he'd have to help. We literally folded our son into the car and went to Children's Hospital. It never occurred to us to call for an ambulance.

On Wednesday when he was admitted, we were told that we could probably take him home that night. The doctors said Roger was dehydrated, would likely respond to treatment, and did not seem sick enough to admit. That day I was presenting a paper at a conference. The director of my department said that one of my colleagues could read it for me if I did not want to leave Roger. Since I had worked hard on the paper and was pleased with it, I wanted to present it myself. Furthermore, the conference was close to the hospital. I said I thought I could take a couple of hours away from the hospital to do this and did, feeling guilty. I thought, however, that there was little I could do for Roger at that point.

When I got back to the hospital, the resident told me Roger had to be admitted because he was cyanotic. This meant that his skin took on a bluish coloration, a condition caused by insufficient oxygen to the blood. The doctors were working him up for cardiac problems.

"Cardiac problems? He had an upset stomach."

The resident said, "There is a heart problem. We're not sure exactly what the problem is, but it is serious."

Our doctor met us and said Roger's situation was worse than he had thought. By that time, Bob had returned to the hospital and we both went up to see Roger. He was hooked up to machines that monitored him. Then the cardiologist came into his room and said that the problem was a heart infection. They were trying to decide what course of action to take.

Bob and I went home that night feeling anxious and confused. Everything had happened very fast. Roger was still being worked up the next day, so I decided to visit my father. While I was trying to help him, I got a call to the nurse's station. It was our pediatrician.

"Roger's gravely ill. You have to come to the hospital right away."

"How bad is he?" I asked.

"He's seriously ill."

"How ill? Is he going to die?"

"He might not make it."

I was stunned. I said a quick good-bye to my father, who seemed bewildered by my hasty departure, and took off for the hospital. On the way, I kept thinking about this strange turn of affairs. How could my baby die before my father? What did all this mean? What did we do wrong? Should we have recognized how critical Roger's situation was when we saw him on Saturday? It had only been a few days. Would it have made any difference if I had stayed with him instead of leaving to give my paper? What a frightening ride that was back to the hospital! I was tearful and tremulous all the way and should not have been driving.

Once I returned, the resident again spoke to me. "We have finally decided that Roger has a staph aureus infection in his aorta. He needs surgery immediately. We expect him to survive the surgery, but probably his chance for long-term survival is less than five percent."

What were we to do? How could we make these decisions? Heart surgery sounded very ominous to us but it seemed to be so urgent. We did not know what questions to ask. The doctors decided to replace his aortic valve with a porcine valve the next day. The attending physician was quiet and compassionate; we placed our confidence in him. We felt we had no choice; this was life or death for Roger, our twenty year old, and we wanted to give him every chance for life.

Meanwhile, we called the other children and Bob's sister, Jo, and brother-in-law, Bob Asher. They came immediately to be with us. I asked our pediatrician what we should do. He said, "You're in the best place for cardiac care. I'd go along with whatever they recommend." We did. It was all a blur. We also called a cousin, who was a thoracic surgeon and tried to explain the best we could what was going on. He said from what he understood we were doing the right thing and that our cardiac surgeons were world-renowned. From then on he or his brother-in-law, an internist, called to check with us every night for the next two months. Another cousin, a pediatrician, also was helpful. We needed guidance even to know what questions to ask.

Once Roger had his first surgery, I could not leave him for very long. Since the hospital gave parents cots if they wanted to spend the night, I began to do this. Occasionally, when he seemed fairly stable, I went home to my own bed but slept fitfully. Fortunately, the hospital staff was incredibly kind and made lots of accommodations for us. Bob continued to work but I really could not. I had to be there, on the premises, so I stayed. For a few hours I went back to the hospital where I worked to supervise but otherwise I took sick time. If these were not legitimate sick days, I was certainly mentally under the weather. I was rarely ill and had accrued many hours of sick time.

Thus began seven weeks of hell. There were seven operations in all – five open-heart surgeries and two abdominal, because of the wide spread infection which never responded to antibiotics. I was told that the aortic valve is not vascular and therefore does not respond to antibiotics. It did, however, shoot the infection to all parts of his body.

The cardiologists were wonderful, caring, sympathetic, competent physicians, who often were called in the middle of the night for another crisis. We were grateful to be in their care. The general surgeons, however, were a different matter. The infection had become systemic, and Roger needed to have abdominal surgery. This meant that he was transferred to the surgical floor with a new team of physicians and nurses who did not know him or us. After only a day, Roger was transferred back to the cardiac ICU but the surgical team was still following him. One day as they came by on their rounds, the chief surgical resident stood by Roger's bed and said among other things, "This 20 year old young man will not recover from this invasive infection." I could hardly believe my ears.

They ignored my presence; I was furious. I accosted them as they were leaving, and said, "Roger can still hear you. It is neither helpful nor therapeutic to talk about him at his bedside in these terms. This is cruel. You can do your teaching away from the bedside."

The resident was very angry and unapologetic. He only glared at me and left precipitously. To my knowledge he did not do this again. Meanwhile, the ICU nurses cheered.

While he was recovering from this surgery, Roger was delirious. I spent long, painful hours holding his hand and trying to soothe him. I could do little else. Once Roger began to talk in a panicked voice, "Help me, help me, I'm falling down a long dark tunnel – it's very black – hold my hand – pull me out, help me, help me!" I was distraught. I held him the best I could and tried to reassure him but his words still haunt me. He knew more than I or any of the physicians did.

During Roger's time in the hospital, he was in and out of consciousness and on and off respirators. It was hard to communicate and certainly almost impossible to have any meaningful conversation but there would be little blips of lucidity. Once when Roger was in the ICU, our friends and next-door neighbors, the Griesses, came to visit. Ro was very comfortable in hospitals and went in to see Roger with me. When Roger saw her, instead of greeting her he said, "Where's Bob?" I think Ro was disappointed but she went out to get her husband with whom Rog had a special relationship. He was clear enough at that moment to note Bob's absence.

Roger had other visitors too. Some of his friends from BU came and after their visit sponsored a blood drive in Roger's behalf at BU. We were quite impressed with their caring and generosity.

To Roger's surprise and delight, his old buddy and forever playmate came down from Colby College to see him. That particular afternoon Roger was more alert than he had been. Luckily they had a good visit, but his friend, Adam Levin, was distressed and dismayed. He had never seen anyone so sick and attached to monitors with tubes running in and out. I think it was Roger's eerie appearance and subdued affect that disturbed Adam so deeply. When you're nineteen or twenty it's devastating and threatening to see someone your own age so very ill. That was the last day that Roger was responsive.

All in all Roger had three aortic valve replacements, a mitral valve replacement, two other open-heart surgeries, two abdominal surgeries for the rampant infection and pancreatitis. He also suffered several strokes and gangrene on his fingers and toes. One night I called the hospital to see how things were going.

"Oh, everything is O.K. We just gave him his insulin shot."

"Insulin shot," I exclaimed. "He never had diabetes."

"Sometimes when the body is under great stress, the pancreas goes out of whack. He's really all right. The insulin is the least of his problems."

There seemed to be no end to the complications. And with each new event the big question for me was will he survive? If he does, what will the quality of his life be? Will he ever be normal again? How will I handle whatever happens? What will my life be like? Will I be able to cope?

This was a period where we were completely dependent on doctors' decisions. There were many specialists consulted; we were in a top medical facility. Our son's life was at stake. Only one of our physician cousins gently suggested that we stop trying. But there was absolutely no question in my mind or Bob's that we had to do everything possible to enable Roger to live. When you are in the world of hospitals and your child is unable to participate in any decision-making or even to understand what is happening to him, you have to keep trying – or at least we did. I do not believe we were able to think clearly or even to process all the information we were given. We had to rely on the professionals; we felt they were doing the best they could.

After his final surgery, Roger lay in the cardiac ICU on a respirator with two nurses in constant attention. His chest looked like a map with all the marks and lines for his tubes. I was able to "bag him" when they were changing his tubes. That process was literally placing a small black balloon type syringe over his mouth and rhythmically squeezing it while he was off the respirator. At least this made me feel I was doing something constructive. It all came to no avail, however, when we were finally called into one of the ICU rooms to meet with the whole team of Roger's cardiac physicians, consultants and nurses.

"We've done all we can. We are so sorry but Roger really isn't breathing any more. What you see on the monitor is the medication keeping him breathing but we cannot get him off the respirator. He cannot breath on his own. We need to disconnect the respirator."

The doctors were crying, the nurses were crying and Bob and I certainly were crying. I remember saying, "I thank you for your efforts. You did all that was humanly possible. Roger has been through too much. He put up a valiant fight but I think it's over. The infection was too much for him. I remember being there when he was born and now I want to be there when he has his final moments."

I called Goldie, Bob's mother, to tell her that the equipment was going to be removed and that Roger was going to die and that in fact he was already dead. "Please do not come to the hospital. Bob, Martha and I want to be alone with him. We'll call you later with the details and plans."

The three of us went into the ICU. There Roger lay – his face nicely shaved his now thin body inert. All of a sudden, Goldie appeared. I was furious; I was not kind. After I had explicitly told her not to come, she did anyway. She was not as close to Roger as she was to the other children. Even though he was sweet and rather courtly with her, he was always different and did not meet her standards. She never bothered to try to understand his problems. I really did not want her there and cried out, "Get her out of here!"

Martha said, "I'll take care of Grandma." She led Goldie out of the room and thus was not with us when Roger took his last breath.

Gradually the nurses removed the awful tubes. They disconnected the respirator. We watched the lines on the monitors go flat as we held Roger's hands, soothed his brow and told him we loved him and that now his troubles would be over.

It was not a glorious ending to his difficult life. It's not fair that he had to endure so much pain, struggle and humiliation. But he showed us courage, determination, spirit, humor and love. We're glad he was part of our lives and we miss him every day, even now so many years later.

Roger died November 18, 1978. Bob and I went to the funeral home to make the same arrangements we had made only six weeks earlier for my father. The extended family gathered and joined our friends and Roger's at the large funeral. We sat *shiva* but were in a daze. Relatives came from across the country; friends brought meals. I'm not sure we could even appreciate everyone who reached out to us. Roger's friends, teachers, neighbors, hospital nurses, our friends all came to offer support. There is always the unreality and finality of death which is so hard to accept. Rituals helped but not totally. We talked about Roger and tried to celebrate his life but had trouble accepting that we had lost our youngest child.

Bob and I returned to work the following week. Each of us found the familiar structure of going back to our usual routines helped us have a sense of normalcy. But nothing felt normal.

After so many days and nights in the hospital, being fully absorbed in Roger's medical crises and finally understanding that his life was really over, we were depleted. There was a great hole for us. We'd go to work, be with people, do our jobs and then come home to a quiet house. Nothing felt real and we found it hard to navigate through each day.

Eventually we began to feel more like ourselves. We missed Roger's cheery phone calls and having him pop in for a visit, but we had seen and been part of the process of his illness and sadly understood the inevitable.

Right after Roger died I remember walking along the street and thinking all these people are going about their business as if nothing has happened. Don't they know the whole world has changed? It was irrational but I felt I had changed and was less intact. Then there was time at the end of the workday when before Roger had become ill, I had gone everyday to be with my father. Now I was not even able to visit him.

It also was difficult, and yet helpful, listening over and over to people saying they were sorry. We needed to hear people share their stories about Roger and we needed to talk about our last days with him. The food people brought, the hugs, the letters, the calls were all reassuring to us. We learned to understand the value of sitting *shiva* and our need for people. Partly because we had spent such a long time in the hospital, it helped to know we had a community of support and understanding. Nevertheless, we felt diminished, different, set apart from normal life. Our family would no longer be the same.

Furthermore, my experience was the same as Alison Smith, who wrote about her own experience with grief in her book, *Name all the Animals*. For me, too, "things I used to do with ease, without a thought, now left me stunned and troubled, unable to figure out where to begin."[1] For example, I couldn't seem to organize a system for keeping track of the cards, letters, contributions and gifts that came our way. This was a task I would normally have done easily. It was fortunate

---

[1] Smith, Alison. 2004. *Name All the Animals*. New York, NY: Scribner, (p. 36).

that one of my cousins came after the funeral and set up a filing system for us. I was not functional.

As the days and weeks went by, we began to feel a new rhythm and orderliness to our lives. However, it was not too long before another tragedy unfolded. Actually it was only sixteen months later. Let me start at the beginning of Jon's life before we get to his end.

Jonathan, Our Middle Son

Jonny is the child I did not know as well as the others. Perhaps it was because he needed me least and therefore got less attention than his older and younger brothers. He was considerate of others, independent, spirited, funny, bright and engaging. Since he was popular and had many close friends, he had a full life outside of the family. Jonny seemed to adopt our values and fit into the rhythm of the family easily. This made life more manageable for everyone. Although he certainly had his moments of adolescent rebellion, he never pushed us as hard as Mark. Neither did he have the many problems Roger had. He was just a good happy kid who was curious, liked to learn and to do well. We enjoyed him.

His beginning was dramatic. While I thought I had arranged for help, no one was around the day my water slowly broke. I called my doctor who said to go immediately to the hospital. That would have been fine except that I was home alone with Mark, 3, and Martha, 2. In desperation, I called my mother-in-law, Goldie. She said, "I'll come but think I'll do my marketing on the way." I was upset and nervous that she would not come on time so I called Bob to ask him to meet all of us at the hospital. There wasn't enough time for him to come home to get me. Since it was a Friday afternoon, I was concerned about getting stuck in traffic. Obviously, I was not thinking clearly at the time.

As I was loading Mark and Martha into the car, Goldie pulled up and said she had changed her mind and had come over directly. After she helped me get the children out of the car, I kissed them good-bye. "Be good for Grandma," I said, as I waved good-bye again and drove off. It took about a half-hour to reach the hospital and park the car. A half hour after that, we had a new baby boy. Bob and his father arrived about the same time the baby was born and saw me shortly thereafter.

I had a fast, easy natural delivery. Jonathan Maynard Sandman was born April 20, 1956.

He was a big baby, almost 8 and a half pounds, with coppery fuzz on his head, big brown eyes and a tiny button nose. Of all our children, he was the easiest baby, as he slept through the night within six weeks. He also was the only baby born in the spring. It was so much more pleasant to nurse him in the early morning when the house was warm and light.

Although he started out big and nursed well, he did not fill out like the others but instead became wiry, thin, and agile. He quickly lost whatever baby fat he had. Of all the children, he was the cuddliest, though his bones would poke into you as you held him. He loved to be close and sit in our laps reading books, listening to music or just being held. He was inquisitive, playful, sweet and funny.

Martha was intrigued with her new brother and quickly got into the role of being a two- year-old big sister. The two in the middle were of similar temperaments and got along well. Mark seemed to feel Jon was more of an irritant and paid less attention to him. Also Mark had started nursery school and had important things to do.

It seemed to take less time to establish a rhythm in our lives. I was already used to managing two schedules and now that Mark and Martha were essentially on the same timetable, it was not difficult to manage Jonny. Furthermore, he was a good sleeper, either because he really slept or because he "self-soothed". He usually could wait until I got to him. Meanwhile Mark and Martha shared a room so that Jonny could have the nursery.

One morning when Jonny was about six months old, Bob and I awoke very early to hear sounds of hilarity coming from his room. We hurried down the hall where Jonny was on his elbows covered in white dust, the talcum powder his brother and sister had poured on him. About all we could see were his brown eyes and pink mouth. The three children were laughing heartily. We were less amused as we admonished the two culprits and tried to excavate Jonny from the powdery mess which could have been very dangerous but fortunately wasn't. Later when we remembered his very white face, we had to suppress our own giggles at this silly bit of mischief.

When Jonny was about fifteen months old, we decided we needed a bigger home. After a long search we found a thirteen-room house in

Waban. We fell in love with the house though it was larger than we needed and more money than we could easily afford. It had a huge den with a cathedral ceiling and a mammoth fieldstone fireplace. The walls were covered in knotty pine with built in bookcases on three sides. The house was on a cul-de-sac on a quiet U shaped street with little traffic. It was a wonderful home in which to raise our children and one we grew to enjoy. We lived there for forty-three years.

Over the years, our family has always enjoyed our camping trips. We first took Jonny to Nickerson State Park, in Brewster on Cape Cod, when he was two. On this first camping trip, Jonny did not like the sand, the bed, the food or anything else. Furthermore his loud complaints made the rest of us embarrassed and miserable. After giving it a try for a few days, we gave in and came home. Because the other two children were disappointed, we got a baby-sitter to stay with Jonny at Goldie's house and took the others to Ogunquit, Maine where we rented a primitive little cabin. It rained the entire time we were there but we all had fun playing board games, doing puzzles and going out for hot dogs, hamburgers and ice cream. Furthermore, back in Newton, Jonny got the undivided attention of his grandparents, which he liked a lot.

One evening when Jonny was in nursery school, the family was sitting around the dining room table and we were all laughing. That night Bob's sister Jo was with us for dinner. I commented to Jo that I thought Jonny was trying to read. "Let's see," she said. I left the table to get a simple book that Jonny had not yet seen. We gave it to him and asked if he could read it. I don't remember the name of the book but he easily read it aloud and then said, "This is a ridiculous book!" which of course it was. However, he had taught himself to read. When we all clapped and voiced our praise, he beamed.

Before he went to nursery school, I participated in leading a playgroup with four other mothers. We took turns picking up the children, bringing them to our respective homes, organizing play activities, songs and snacks and returning them to their own homes a few hours later. Three year olds, as I discovered for the third time, have a very short attention span. We had play dough, papers, crayons, puzzles, stories and snacks, but time always seemed to go by very quickly. What I had planned for even fifteen minutes turned out to last for about three. In addition, by that time I had Roger, who at six months needed a nap or to be fed or changed in the midst of the other programs. To complicate matters, Roger would invariably fall asleep just as it was time to load the others into the station wagon to go home. The best part was that I only had the children for one day a week. The other four days I could pay undivided attention to Roger.

Jonny was not a talker until he was three. But unlike Mark who was quiet and Martha who had a lot to say, Jonny was a screamer. He would point and say some gobble-de-gook. "Try it again, Jonny", we'd say. He would but we still could not understand. Then he'd screech. He was frustrated but so were we. Fortunately once he learned to talk, he became more biddable and pleasant and had a lot to say.

In elementary school, Jonny was a quick learner and eager to participate in music, sports and plays. He loved to dress up and pretend to be a lion or a caveman or whatever was on his mind. It did not have to be Halloween – he just liked to play, to try on different personae. Then in second grade he became disinterested in his schoolwork and began to be silly in class. His teacher was concerned about his behavior. Eventually she decided he was bored. He did not like to read for pleasure; he read for information. Fortunately, his teacher found some science books for him and he soon was lost in books he enjoyed and could talk about. He impressed people with his knowledge of facts that interested him, if not anyone else. Furthermore, he settled down in school.

Around third grade, we took him to get an ice cream cone. He could not seem to decide which flavor he'd have. "For heaven's sake, Jonny, make up your mind," I said. Usually after deliberating for a while, he'd choose vanilla anyway.

He looked a bit sad and then said "I can't read the flavors." That was how we knew he needed glasses. When he got them he was excited. "I didn't realize you could see individual leaves on the trees." "People in the movies really have faces!" What a revelation!

Jonny began playing clarinet when he was eight. At first he took lessons in school. Then we had to find a private teacher for him. Luckily a friend, who taught grade school in Newton and was a clarinetist, said she'd be interested in teaching him. To make it easier for me, she came to our house in the late afternoon for several years. Then, while Jonny had his lesson, our dog Willie howled. The clarinet hurt his ears. To make things manageable, we had to keep Willie in the kitchen during lesson and practice time. Later Jonny also played tenor saxophone. He really liked participating in orchestras which he continued to do in high school and college.

When he was nine, Jonny was sledding and cracked his scalp, which bled profusely. We took him to the hospital where the surface wound was stitched. A large, spectacular pressure bandage was wrapped around his skull. The bandage looked like a white helmet. "I feel fine," Jonny said. Since there was no concussion and there were no restrictions, we decided he could come with us for our planned trip to Beacon Hill. As we walked through Boston looking at the Christmas decorations, strangers either stared at him or came over, clucking about how dreadful it was that he hurt his head. He then got to tell them about his mishap and loved the attention he received.

Around the same time in the summer, we had many letters from camp, a few of which I saved. One begins: "I threw up Saturday night on my beans so I don't have to eat beans anymore." Another said, "We hiked up Red Hill but one kid almost fainted. I sure didn't. We had deviled ham. I hated it." Still another began "Hello, Mudah, Hello Fada. Not much to say but I have to write the required Sunday letter." Typical letters from camp, but we felt they were high-spirited and that he was having a good time.

In fifth grade, he wrote his autobiography and fairly described his family:

> "I have an older brother and sister and a younger
> brother. My older brother of course has always bullied me
> around. I do too, to my little brother but I sometimes can
> be nice to him when I'm in the mood. I get along alright
> with my sister."

When Jon was in sixth grade he had to respond to this assigned problem: "An airplane was about to crash but only one passenger could be saved. Who do you think it should be?" Most of the kids chose politically important people – George Washington, Abraham Lincoln, Martin Luther King, Jr. Jon chose a pregnant woman. When questioned about his choice he said, "If you save a pregnant woman, you save two lives." Both his teacher and we thought that was quite astute. Jonny was a thinker and not much of a talker but when he felt clear about an issue, he expressed it well. Because he rarely shared his feelings, it was interesting and informative for us to learn how perceptive he could be.

Although Jonny read early and comprehensively, he seldom read for pleasure or at least did not read stories or novels unless they were assigned. As we learned when he was in second grade, he preferred to read for information and continued to spend hours pouring over the World Book Encyclopedia or the National Geographic or even Popular Mechanics. He loved impressing us with the valuable bits of trivia he had gleaned from his readings. In that way, he was much like Bob who, we always teased, was full of useless information.

Probably from his reading science magazines, Jonny developed a passion for animals, especially snakes. "I'm going to be a herpetologist or a venomologist," he asserted. We weren't sure if he was really interested or was just trying to impress us that he knew these names but we learned that he really was serious. He already had an iguana and a tiny baby alligator but he really wanted a snake. Therefore, with his own money he bought a boa constrictor that lived in his room in an old aquarium with sand on the bottom. We put meshed wire over the top and weighted it with rocks. Jon understood that I had no interest in caring for this snake and that it was totally his responsibility.

The boa did very little. It was about four and a half feet long and left little mess. But it needed to be fed and what it ate was live mice. I not only did not like snakes but I hated mice. In the beginning, Jonny used his allowance to buy the mice. A mouse cost twenty-five cents and the boa ate one a week. In fact, the whole neighborhood came to watch the feeding. Even today some of the neighborhood boys say that one of their most vivid childhood memories was getting up their courage to watch the boa eat the mouse.

After a while Bob suggested that the snake might be better satisfied with a rat – a more substantial meal, which might last as long as two mice. They bought the rat and put it in the cage with the boa. Everyone watched but it was pathetic. The rat cowered in one corner and the boa curled up in the other. Nothing happened. Each was terrified of the other. Eventually Bob said, "Let's take the rat back and exchange it for two mice."

One mouse was consumed immediately and before we knew it, the other mouse had produced a litter of fourteen babies. That was the beginning of the end. The babies grew rapidly and began reproducing. Their geometric progression was alarming. Soon Jonny had about five cages of mice – many more than the boa could handle. It also meant he

32

had to clean all those containers. My fears, however, were that we'd soon have little white mice escaping. So, how did he deal with the problem? Jonny began selling his mice to any pet store that would take them. The radius for pet stores kept getting larger and larger.

One morning Jonny came into our room announcing, "The boa's not in its cage." I panicked and so did Jon, but for different reasons.

"You have to find it," I said. "I'm not going to be in this house with a loose snake. You can't go to school until the boa is back in its cage."

The hunt began. Jonny finally found the boa clinging vertically to a wall in a dark corner of his closet. He put it back in its container, placed heavier weights on the grating and went to school. Later we called the Museum of Science. They suggested we place a shoebox with a hole in its side in the aquarium. Then the boa could slink into it and feel secure in its dark, cozy place. The boa did not escape again.

At one point, we all were going away and did not know what to do with the livestock. Our neighbor offered to take care of the "pets". We were grateful for the offer. When a long line of the boa, mice, iguana, alligator and fish were presented to our friends, they wondered what they had gotten themselves into. I think they would have preferred caring for the dog, which we were able to put in a kennel. It was not long after that Jonny decided to sell the boa and the mice. The alligator and the iguana died and we were left with the fish and the dog. At least the dog had a personality, was responsive and most of all was Jonny's confidant.

When Jonny was at summer camp, we went to see him on visiting day. "Don't forget Willie!" we heard over and over. So on visiting day, we took Wilhelm von Waban, the dachshund, to visit him. Jonny was so excited he hardly acknowledged our being there but went to hug and kiss his pet. We should have known how much Willie meant to him. Everyday the dog knew just what time to sit at the window and wait for the kids to come home from school. And when they came through the door there was great excitement as the dog and children, especially Jonny, greeted each other.

There was only one problem with Willie. He was vicious around food. The family knew not to bother him when he was eating but visitors did not. And Willie would bite. One day he escaped from our house and visited a barbecue nearby. There he snapped at a small child. The child was frightened but not hurt. Nevertheless we felt responsible, both for not knowing where the dog was and for what he did.

Since we had small children in and out of our house and Willie was excitable, it felt like he was more of a liability than we wanted. Eventually, much to everyone's chagrin, we found a new home for Willie with some people who lived in a calmer environment in the country. We had discussed the need for finding Willie a new home with the children but it was not real for them until they actually came home from school. Not only Willie, but also his bowl, leash, bed and toys were gone. While the other children were sorrowful and angry with us for actually giving Willie away, Jonny was distraught. He became tearful (rare for him) ran to his room and sobbed for a long time. He hardly spoke a word that whole day. It was a sad day for us all to feel the emptiness of Willie's departure but it was hardest for Jonny.

Toward the end of sixth grade, because he was so bright and eager to learn, we felt Jonny would profit from a private school. We thought a school like Roxbury Latin would be stimulating for him. Jon was ambivalent. The application came and before we could deal with it, Jonny had written his essay about his most meaningful experience. He began by saying, "One day, me and my father went fishing..." I was distressed. If we had been able to supervise he would have said, "One day my father and I went fishing," but there it was in ink and there wasn't much we could do about it. He was rather cavalier about the whole application. For example, in response to the question of whether he was ever tutored and if so why, he answered, "I was tutored in Hebrew because my mother is a social worker." This of course was not the whole story. Since I was still in graduate school, I could not arrange car pools for Hebrew School. Therefore we arranged for a tutor to come to our house. At any rate, he was accepted. The headmaster said they were quite sure Jon had written his own application.

We actually did not understand how stressful it was for him at Roxbury Latin until late in the year. He seemed to be taking everything in stride, did his homework systematically, received top grades, excelled in rope climbing and participated in all sports including football and wrestling. He did not even seem to mind the dress code requiring jackets and ties. But all that year he had terrible hives. At the end of the summer he said, "I don't want to go back to Roxbury Latin. I miss my friends. I miss girls. I want to be in public school." We contacted the headmaster who assured us that Jon would do well wherever he went to school.

In the spring of his year at Roxbury Latin, when Jon was thirteen, he was playing baseball and unfortunately got in the way of the bat after the batter hit the ball. He was knocked unconscious and rushed to the hospital. We had gone out for the evening but the sitter contacted us and we went directly to the hospital. Jonny did not know who or where he was.

"What's your name?"

"Robbie."

"Oh, do you know what town you live in?"

"Baltimore."

It was scary. We did not know what the damage was or if he would be O.K. We understood he had had a concussion but no one could assure us that he would fully recover. That whole evening he was disoriented. When he seemed calmer and slept, we decided to go home. It was clear he needed to be supervised and stay in the hospital. By the next day, he was reoriented but was instructed to stay in bed. When we came to visit, he was doing pull-ups from the curtain rod over his bed.

"What are you doing? You're supposed to be quiet and in bed."

"I'm not off the bed. I have to get some exercise," he said. Although we were annoyed with him for testing his limits, we were also amused and relieved. If he was up to that we assumed he would recover.

I remember having mixed emotions about Jonny's returning to public school. He had been getting a superior education at Roxbury Latin, a school with high academic standards. In seventh grade the teachers did not assume anything. They systematically started with the basics and progressed from there. For example, in English they began by writing sentences, then paragraphs, then whole compositions. The same was true for sports. Each boy had to learn the basics of the sport he was doing before he went on to play the sport. The school also emphasized being courteous and having respect for their teachers and fellow students. While we approved of these methods and values, we also wanted our son to be happy and he wasn't. It should be added that neither Bob nor I felt totally comfortable with the intellectual elitism that we found there. Later, when Jonny was in high school, he commented that if he had stayed at Roxbury Latin he probably would have had a better education.

So Jon went back to public school in September. He never had hives again. He also returned determined to be at the top of his class. Since he had only studied Latin at Roxbury Latin, he was behind his friends in French. Nevertheless, he insisted on joining the eighth grade French class and by the end of the term already excelled in French without getting special help. He clearly had made the right decision for himself.

When he was in eighth grade his Social Studies teacher told us Jon had complained to her. He said he worked hard to get his papers in on time and he thought it was not fair to have to wait a long time to get them back. Furthermore, he felt he couldn't learn as much from the teacher's feedback when the paper was stale. His teacher was impressed and told him he was right. She then said to us that she might not return all the papers quickly but she would try to get Jon's back to him fast. We were pleased that he could be so assertive and also delighted with the teacher's sensitive response.

Around this time, Jonny decided he wanted to earn some money. One opportunity for him was to "peddle" *The Phoenix*, a weekly publication. He got the papers and went into Boston to sell them. When he came home, we asked him how he did. "I don't think this is a very good business," he replied.

"Why not?"

"Well, it was a long hot day and I got tired and thirsty and then I got hungry too, so I bought a bagel and a coke and then a sandwich and I had to pay for the "T" and suddenly all the profits were eaten up!" Thus his business career ended!

* * *

For Jon's Bar Mitzvah we had to get him a suit. We already had gone through a big scene with Mark a few years before. Mark did not want a suit and resisted it loudly and tearfully. Of course, he never wore the suit again. We told Jon he had to wear the suit only once and that we'd get it altered to fit him. A good sport, he said, "O.K. I'll wear it. It doesn't matter to me!" The jacket fit adequately but the pants had to be taken in so much to accommodate his skinny body that the two back pockets met at the seam. Jon, however, didn't seem to care.

As with Mark, both his grandfathers and his father were with him as the Torah was passed from generation to generation. Jon conducted the service well and seemingly effortlessly. As usual he belittled his achievements and brushed off the compliments, but we were very proud of him.

In high school, Jonny liked soccer and swimming but he loved to ski. For many years, we had family trips to ski areas. At that time, Bob was building electronic controls for ski lifts and often got passes for the family while he worked on the equipment. Eventually, we were able to rent a ski house from our good friends the Levins, so we could ski more regularly at Waterville Valley. This was quite a boon since there were many beds and the kids could bring friends. It might have been difficult to get Jon up for school but on ski trips he was up at dawn and raring to go. In fact, he liked to ski better than anything and was a smooth, graceful, controlled skier, who quickly graduated to advanced slopes. We enjoyed seeing him glide down the mountain, his long skinny body in tune with his surroundings. When he was skiing, he glowed and exuded a sense of well-being and accomplishment that he may have felt on other occasions but rarely displayed.

We have almost no serious pictures of Jon. He was always fooling around, his beaming or mugging face in the corner of many pictures. Just as he liked to dress up when he was little, he also loved to act or to "ham it up" when he was in high school. He was eager to don a costume, to be someone else, to get attention. Therefore, in a high school production of *Zorba the Greek*, he delighted in his costume and make-up for his comical role as a wily old man. In addition, in the same play, he was also an altar boy, which involved another costume. His performance was great and we were thrilled by his "moment of stardom".

In high school, he valued his independence and his many good friends, so in his adolescent years he was out a lot when we were trying to deal with the problems of our other boys. Roger embarrassed him. They looked much alike – both were well over six feet, had bright red hair, white skin with freckles and wore horn-rimmed glasses. But Roger was different from other kids – awkward, not popular, not good-looking, not a good student and not always appropriate in his behavior. It was hard for Jon to have his brother tag along and Jon often tried to dissociate from him. As soon as he could, Jonny got contact lenses, partly for sports, but mainly, we felt, to look unlike his brother.

For a time, they shared the same large room but they were so different temperamentally that they were not good roommates. Jon was organized and neat; Roger was not. Jon did his homework while Roger always needed prodding and help to complete his work. There was practically a line of demarcation between the two sides of their room.

While Roger's habits were annoying, Jon did not tease him. He knew Roger wasn't like other kids and seemed to accept that fact. Still, he wanted his privacy and to be apart. Because Roger idolized his brother, it became even harder for Jon to complain about him. After a few years, Roger moved to another bedroom. This change helped them be better brothers. Then Jon was more accepting of Roger's idiosyncrasies.

In his junior year of high school, Jon dislocated a disc in his back. He was hospitalized and had traction as well as many uncomfortable tests. Nothing worked. Since his situation was acute, surgery was recommended and he had the disc removed.

* * *

Afterward, he was never the same cheerful guy. He did not recover well and continued to have severe back spasms. On a visit to his doctor, we asked if a back brace might help. The doctor said, "That sounds like a good idea." He also said that because of Jonny's build, it would probably take a very long time for him to heal since nerves regenerate slowly. It was a grim report and prognosis.

We tried to do what we could to make things easier for Jonny but his pain persisted. In desperation, we consulted with a physiatrist in New York who made a few suggestions. Essentially, however, Jonny continued to be uncomfortable. After this, while he kept up with his studies, he seemed to lose his drive to excel both in high school and thereafter. Even in college he seemed satisfied to be a B student and did not want or have the energy to push himself harder.

By his senior year in high school Jon wanted to go to Dartmouth. He was accepted at many colleges but not at Dartmouth. This was particularly hard on him, since one of his friends had been accepted with lower class rank, lower SAT scores and fewer honors courses. This made him feel that all his efforts did not matter. Eventually Jon enrolled at Middlebury College. During one of his breaks freshman year, he brought home some friends. At breakfast, these young men sat around the table and one of them said jokingly, "Well, here we are. Ivy League rejects!" It's too bad they felt that way. Why should the Ivy Leagues matter? I suppose I also was angry that while I knew that each college had its own criteria for admission, it was often hard to understand why one student was accepted over another.

The summer after his freshman year he went to Bartending School and then got a job at Tony's Italian Villa as the bartender. One night,

Bob and I decided to patronize the restaurant and first went into the bar, so that Jon could serve us. Neither of us had ever gone to a bar. We ordered our drinks – wine for me and a gin and tonic for Bob and sat at a small table. When Jon served the drinks we sipped them and tried to make conversation but it felt awkward. Eventually, we paid our tab, tipped our server generously and left. Later that night Jon's comment to us was, "Gee, you two don't even know how to behave in a bar!" He was right.

At the end of the summer, he visited his college friend Rich who lived in Hawaii and wrote:

"I went snorkeling at Puako – Rich's brother Neil caught a wild sheep with a bow and arrow! We watched him skin it and we ate it – good tasting – I stood at South Point, the southernmost place in the USA – we went to Volcano Park. Sulfur fumes really get you – we went into the rain forest up in the mountains where we picked maile – a sweet smelling vine used for leis – we also went swimming in a pond fed by a big waterfall on the slopes of Kahala. It was freezing – the water had a brown color due to fern spores – we went hiking in the Polulu Valley. The steep trail is just on the side of the cliffs. We walked behind an enormous waterfall. The scenery is like something out of *King Kong*. Me and Rich (he never got the grammar right) had a rotten guava fight – they just explode their slimy goo all over you on impact. We washed off in a cool irrigation ditch built by coolies at the turn of the century."

Clearly he saw his experience as an exotic adventure; he appreciated the natural beauty as well as the hospitality of his hosts. Bob and I delighted in his excitement.

After his sophomore year at Middlebury College Martha, Roger, Bob and I went to bring him home. The four of us were lugging his stuff from his room to the car while he was holding court, joking with his friends and flirting with the girls. It actually was rare for him not to offer to help, but this time he was charming and happy as he entertained his buddies. I don't think it occurred to us to ask him to participate. I also don't believe we had seen Jon play center stage in this way. We were probably awed. Afterward we wondered, not only how he could have been so oblivious to what we were doing but also that we let him take advantage of us. It wasn't long before we realized what it was: he was charismatic. He charmed not only his friends, but also us.

Jon spent the first semester of his junior year at Goldsmith College in the University of London. There he took mainly science courses as he was majoring in biology. He also enjoyed the pubs (he really enjoyed the pubs!), being on his own and making new friends. He took the following semester off and just backpacked around Europe, sometimes alone and sometimes with a friend. What letters we received! – Full of his observations and experiences.

For instance, before he took off for winter break he wrote:

> "The Christmas Party at Goldsmith College turned out
> well. I got an award (third place for the gourmet of the year
> because of my voracious appetite by Limey standards). I
> think I deserved first place!"

We were amused because skinny Jon was famous in our household for having a big appetite. It reminded us of the time he slept very late and came down for his usual hearty breakfast. As he finished, he looked at the clock and said, "My goodness, it's after twelve. It's time for lunch." And he proceeded to devour the next meal without leaving the table.

Also from Goldsmith he described his zoology class by saying:

> "Next week we will dissect a mink. They don't use latex
> injected and preserved specimens; instead it will be a
> freshly killed and skinned animal."

This certainly was not a frog or the usual cat in his anatomy classes, so he was intrigued. Was he repulsed? We do not know, but it was a new experience he wanted to share.

When he left college, he hitchhiked around and frequently wrote of his travels. For example, from Ireland we received this note:

> "The hostels were only 60 pence a night. There is good
> traditional folk music here as well as fine weather. A guy
> let me stay at his place in Mayo for a couple of days. There
> was no running water, no electricity and for cooking just a
> peat fireplace."

Then, later in Marseilles, some fisherman offered him a wonderful fish soup – clearly an authentic bouillabaisse that was special enough for him to write about. He spoke French fluently, which held him in good stead on his travels.

He seemed particularly to enjoy his adventures in Greece. He wrote:

"We stayed on the Island of Crete – As far as ruins are concerned I saw Knossos and Paros. They are pretty ruined ruins – the cost of living was low and we spent very little money, sleeping on beaches and eating bread, olives and feta cheese."

Later in Crete he wrote he was traveling with a friend from Bowdoin and said:

"For the first time we have rented a room in a hotel for $2 a night. It was good to have a real shower and a chance to wash our clothes. We've been hiking almost everywhere, meaning plenty of exercise and camping on beaches. For two nights we slept in a cave!! Sometimes we hitchhiked – We've so far been hitting all the small towns, trying to get away from the tourists (which is pretty hard). People can really be friendly and despite the language barrier, it's fun trying to communicate."

He commented to us in one letter that there were very few young women. To his dismay, they seemed to be protected from these wandering Americans. As usual from his letters, he was being frugal and determined to make his way on his own, although he knew we would help if he needed it. Part of the adventure for him was to see how far he could make his dollars go.

We were eagerly awaiting a letter or call to tell us when Jonny would be coming home when one day as I was working at my desk in our kitchen, I looked out the glass door and saw a scraggy Jon.

As I opened the door, I couldn't believe my eyes. I hugged him and then said, "Why didn't you let us know you were coming? We wanted to meet you at the airport. How did you get home?"

"Oh, I took the T. I wanted to surprise you". So there he was, slightly heavier and needing a shave and haircut; he was dirty but he stood in front of me with his charming grin and twinkling eyes, and an assertion of his independence. I was delighted to have him home.

Returning to Middlebury, however, was a difficult transition for him. He was now out of sync with his friends and said he wanted to live alone in an apartment in town. Eventually he found one near a river where he could also fish, which was his way of relaxing. His last year at Middlebury was hard. He was not happy and did not do very well. Furthermore, that was also the year Roger died. Although Jonny never talked to us very much about his feelings, I'm sure Roger's death was awful for him. We called to keep him informed about Roger's condition and he drove from Middlebury a few times during Roger's illness to see him, often disconcerting the nursing staff who saw someone looking very similar to Roger walking around the hospital.

When we phoned to say Roger had finally died, he called back in a panic to say he couldn't find his car keys. Fortunately, we knew we had placed a spare key under the front bumper (the car had been my father's, who had died a few weeks before Roger did). Jon found the key and came home for the funeral.

Although we knew Jonny was hurting, he couldn't or wouldn't talk. Later we learned from his girl friend that he felt sad that he had not been a better brother to Roger. He felt guilty because he had not been closer and kinder to his little brother, yet said very little to us about his feelings.

After the funeral in November, he returned to Middlebury. For his January term, we felt he needed some fun and adventure and treated him to study with a Middlebury group in Belize, which he enjoyed. He described it as follows:

> "– The city here is colorful and run down. It is humid
> and hot (100 degrees F). The city has open sewers. We've
> been taking side trips – to a Mangrove Swamp and the
> Savannah. There are lots of birds and we saw footprints of
> fox and armadillos. The guesthouse we're staying in is OK.
> They serve us three meals a day – lobster tails, venison,
> plantains are the more exotic items. Our house is also host
> to one spider monkey, one macaw, four doves, a turtle, five
> dogs, five cats and many geese. So I have much company."

We felt he was taking in the flora and fauna of the area and appreciating the diverse population as well. Furthermore, he still enjoyed sampling new food. While he participated in this January term, it again was hard for him to concentrate on his academics when he returned for his final semester at Middlebury. He was grieving for his brother and worried about what lay ahead for him. Nevertheless, he graduated in 1979.

While he was at Middlebury he had enjoyed the stage band where he played clarinet and tenor saxophone. He had made many close friends but was not sure what he wanted to do with his life. Unlike some students, he was not heading toward medicine or law or business school – he had no career plans. Even though he majored in biology he did not want to pursue further studies in science. He seemed restless, yet was not ready for graduate school since he did not know what he wanted to study. All he was sure of was that he wanted to be independent and did not want to live at home.

Meanwhile, Martha had met Ted Holmes and they moved in together that summer so that Jon was able to take over Ted's bachelor apartment in Cambridge. He then found a job as a salesman for a giftware company. It was a starting position and not what he wanted to do but there were things he could learn, partly about selling himself as well. He was happy and successful. Furthermore he had a lovely girlfriend, Carol.

Jonny 4th Grade

Jon 1973

Jon at Middlebury

Jon and Bob at Middlebury Graduation 1979

Jon's Final Days

⚒

THE last time we saw Jon alive was in Cambridge. At the time we knew he was going to New York the following day for a business convention. It was exciting – "all expenses paid." On a whim I called Jonny and asked if he'd like to join us at La Groceria, an Italian restaurant near him. His first response was, "I don't think so," followed by "Well what the hell, why not?" Luckily we shared a nice meal and a hug good-bye. Then we each took off the next morning – Jon to New York and we to Florida to visit Goldie.

We later learned from his friend Ben Green who lived with his wife in New York that he had invited Jon to spend the night with them. Jon had considered staying with them but decided to come home. The following night was Saturday and Jon's girl friend was working. Since Jon was invited to a party with some friends from his new job, he decided to go. He didn't know any of these people very well.

We don't know a great deal about what happened next except that at two in the morning while we were in Florida with Bob's mother and stepfather, Ted called us from Boston. "Jon's had an accident. He was at a party and apparently fell out a window. There are some very scared kids here at the hospital where Martha and I are. You better speak to the doctor."

The doctor said, "Hello. I'm sorry to tell you that your son has been badly hurt in a fall. He is not responding and his eyes are fixed. He has some broken bones. We have him on life supports now. I think you should come here as quickly as possible."

"We'll be there as soon as we can," we said.

We had trouble making sense of this phone call. When you're not on the scene nothing feels real. However, we'd spoken to Ted and Martha and to a doctor, so something awful was happening. We could hardly wait to get to Boston. My heart was racing and I was tremulous but not tearful. Bob was better able to think clearly in emergencies and managed all the details for our return flight early in the morning. I was a zombie and useless. As we packed, we tried to explain the situation to Goldie and Joseph, her husband, but had little to tell them except that Jon's condition was dire and seemed ominous. Then Joseph took us to the airport for our return trip.

Upon our arrival at Boston City Hospital, we made our way through the maze of hallways to the trauma unit. At the information desk Bob said, "We're here to see Roger Sandman."

"No, it's Jonathan Sandman," I corrected.

It really was *déjà vu* but this time it was hard to find appropriate people and information. When we made our way to the ICU, we finally saw Jonny. He was hooked up to the same machines we had only recently witnessed with Roger. Jonny's body was lying there but in every way he seemed to be absent. Where was our son?

The nurses in the unit were very kind and said they knew Jon was not their usual patient in this big inner city hospital. He was clean — even his fingernails were clean. But there he lay, neatly shaved, warm but inert. He appeared lifeless, without response; no flicker in his big brown eyes, no grin, no animation of any kind.

The nurses introduced us to a resident physician who was not comfortable with us. He said they had put Jonny on life-support machines while they tried to assess his condition.

"Can we speak with an attending physician?" I asked.

"What do you mean?" the resident asked.

"You know," I replied sharply, "a grown-up doctor."

I was annoyed that the very young resident did not empathize with what it's like to have your child in this lifeless state. He did not maintain eye contact and was evasive. We were not comfortable with him.

Eventually an attending did come to talk with to us. He was an older, clearly more experienced physician who was compassionate. He looked directly at us and said, "I'm sorry. We tried to give Jonathan the benefit of the doubt. We're sure there is damage to his hands that, if he recovers, will probably not work properly again but that is not the biggest problem. We think he is not feeling anything. In fact we believe he is brain dead. Therefore we'll have to do three electroencephalograms. If all three come back flat we'll have to make some decisions."

Bob and I were stunned. Could this be possible? It was only sixteen months since Roger had died. What was happening to us? To our family? Here was Jonny, our liveliest, most spirited son, essentially lifeless. We knew nothing of the circumstances of his fall and none of the people who were with him. What was Jonny involved in that we did not know about? Why were we beset with this? Why him? Why us?

Bob talked to the police who said it was just an accident – these things unfortunately happen to kids at parties. But Jonny was not intoxicated nor on drugs. He tested negative for those. I wondered what Jonny had been doing. Was he leaning out the window for some fresh air when he lost his balance? Was he pushed out the window? Was this playful or malicious? It was a cold February night, the ground was frozen but he had not fallen far, only two floors. How long had he been lying there before someone realized he was missing or had fallen? So many unanswered questions. We did not know a soul from the party nor did we hear from any of them. Bob, Martha and Mark went to see where he fell. I could not.

Meanwhile we were trudging into Boston City Hospital, which was a labyrinth of tunnels lined with shabby peeling green walls. We sat in a small, colorless waiting room outside the ICU occasionally going in to see if there were any changes, any signs of life. I called a friend, a prominent surgeon and described the situation. I really wanted Jonny in a different hospital. Our friend checked on Jon's condition, spoke with his physician and then reported that he thought he was in a good trauma unit and that his care was appropriate. Undoubtedly, he knew the prognosis.

Eventually the doctor spoke to Bob and me. I did not want to hear what he had to say.

"We have done three electroencephalograms and there was no brain activity. He is brain dead. We are now sure that your son is being kept alive by machines. I'm afraid that now is the time to turn off the respirator. It's time to say good-bye. I'm sorry."

These words were too awful, too heartbreaking and too sad. But what could we do? Our brightest son, brain dead. Dead. Cause of death: fracture of the skull with brain contusions. I could not accept this.

At first, I couldn't even cry.

It seemed like only minutes later as Bob and I, as well as Mark and

Martha, sat stunned and overwhelmed that another resident whom we did not know came into the waiting room carrying a pile of papers.

"We want his kidneys," he said, "but we have to take them while the machines are still going. Would you sign for this now? Oh, and we could probably use his eyes too."

Bob said, "Could you please give us some time to digest the terrible news we've just received? Leave us alone for a while." The resident was disgruntled as he walked away still carrying his papers.

We conferred with Mark and Martha. There was little doubt that Jonny was dead. I felt we definitely should donate any of his body parts that might be useful to someone else. Bob and the children were less certain. Eventually we decided this was the right path to take and signed the papers.

It was a miserable way to say good-bye. Jonny looked fine; his skin was warm, his long body had no apparent bruises. Even his hands looked intact. But his eyes, fixed open, were lifeless. We each kissed him, rubbed his arms and face and assured him of our love. Finally as we stood by and watched, two orderlies wheeled him out of the ICU as we said good-bye.

When Jonny left, the nurses stood respectfully at a distance. They were compassionate. Each night Jonny was there I had called several times hoping for a change. They were always kind as they related that his condition was the same. Bob and I had sat in the waiting room all day but I did not feel the same need to stay at night as I had with Roger. It really felt to me that Jonny was probably dead on arrival. His accident was on Friday night or early Saturday morning. The machines were turned off on Wednesday, March 5, 1980. He was 23 years old.

We pulled ourselves together the best we could, thanked the nurses and then left to make funeral arrangements. It was unbearably painful and surreal but real at the same time. We had the same awful phone calls to make, had to contact the same funeral home, write an obituary, repeat all the steps we had gone through just a few months before with Roger and with my father. And we did not want to do any of it. We were totally depleted. Jon had been the sunshine in our lives and now he was gone.

This time when the tears began I could not stop them. It was too much. I couldn't sleep, couldn't eat, did not want to talk but then if I started I couldn't stop. We had another large funeral in our temple.

Relatives came from around the country, as did friends. Mark was devastated and more tearful than I'd ever seen him. Martha had Ted. I'm sure she was overwhelmed with these losses too. Jonny was everyone's buddy and made us laugh. For the funeral I wrote a letter to him. In it I described what he had meant to us. Then I gave it to the rabbi to read. The rabbi mentioned it during the service but said he did not think it was appropriate to read. I was disappointed as were many others but perhaps his judgment was better than mine. He never returned the letter and I had no copy. Jonny was much too young for his promising life to end.

His death was particularly hard on Bob. He and Jon were much alike and Bob had had great hopes for this son. Both Bob and I were barely functional. Each of us went back to work after the week of sitting *shiva,* but neither of us was very efficient. Bob in particular noticed that he was pushing papers around and getting little done. This was not his usual way.

It's not clear to me how I was acting. As I drove to work I found myself weeping. The slightest incident would trigger a memory and remind me of our losses. I would see a red-haired young man riding a bike and think, "Oh, there's Jon", and remember Jonny was no more. I would see him at our back door and then blink, shake my head and realize he couldn't have been there. I visited a neighbor whose boys had a tall red-haired guy sitting with his back to me and my immediate response was, "Oh, that's where Jon is," and then remember he was dead. At home I'd wait for a telephone call from Jon or Roger, which I knew was impossible. I felt crazy yet knew my reactions were not abnormal.

Back at work, I think I was able to listen to patients and be useful to them. I certainly did not share my personal experience. In some ways I could hear and feel their pain more than I had in the past. But my colleagues were tiptoeing around me. They were sympathetic but were not sure what to say. If they asked how I was doing I told them – more than they wanted to hear. I talked too much about how deeply I was hurting. On the other hand I tried to do the best I could to put them at ease. I just was out of control a lot of the time. I struggled to put my all into my work during the hours I was there. Then I'd go home to my empty house and all the mundane tasks that I still had to do but that I did not want to do anymore. The house was very quiet and Bob and I had little to say to each other.

51

Soon each of us in the family had some therapy, but separately. In retrospect, we probably should have seen a family therapist and worked things out together but we didn't. We were each encased in our own pain and sorrow. Jonny was the one in the family who seemed to get along with everyone, although he had more trouble with Roger. That's why his death seemed to leave such a terrible hole. In some ways I didn't want to share my own sorrow. I wanted to talk about it as if the losses were mine alone. I did not seem to be able to take care of anyone. My relationship with Bob was strained, too. I withdrew into my misery and myself and certainly was not available to my husband in any way. On the other hand, he wanted and needed to be close to me. I had no wish for sexual intimacy; he needed it. It's to Bob's credit that he hung in with me and onto me. I was not much of a wife to him but he was trying to take care of me and preserve our marriage, which he did.

I wondered why we had children if we were only going to lose them. We had tried so hard to be good parents and to give our kids what they needed as well as the material things that neither Bob nor I had had. We were interested in the children's activities, their schoolwork and their friends. We tried to be available to them and to build a strong, solid family. Why did our boys die? Why was our family so decimated? Nothing made sense.

At first we had a lot of attention. People brought over meals, which were great since I had no interest in cooking or feeding people. Our considerate friends tried to entertain us, feed us, include us. I don't know how much we talked about how we were feeling. We made a big effort not to burden people with our grief or to focus on our losses. We did not want to lose our friends or be too much for them to cope with. Our situation was particularly threatening to anyone with children. We broke their bubble. Bad things can and do happen to good people. We were living proof of that.

I've often wondered why it was Jon I saw in the visualization. Was I feeling guilty that I did not know him better, that I had spent much time and emotional energy on his two brothers, but less on him? He always seemed so self-sufficient and self-directed that he placed few demands on us. Even in his teens when he had his moments of rebellion he never pushed us as far as Mark did. In many ways he seemed to adopt more of our values, or at least more of my values, so I felt I could understand him. He wanted to learn; he did well in school; he had good, constant friends; he was a fine all around kid who was good in sports and music; he was charming and lovable. He also was brightness and laughter for us.

After Jonny died I fell apart more than I did with the others. I could not contain my tears. Jonny's death had no redeeming features. We knew nothing of the circumstances surrounding his fall. I have been and always will be haunted by the unknowns. He had a bright future ahead of him. The world was just opening up for him, and suddenly he was gone. Perhaps this is why he emerged in my visualization. In many ways I had more unfinished business with him and a visceral longing to bring him back.

* * *

I suppose Bob and I had the highest dreams for Jonny. While Bob hoped eventually to have worked with Jon in his business, I was quite sure that was not part of Jon's plans. He was not an engineer like his father and grandfather. He liked archeology, anthropology, geography and geology. He enjoyed speaking French and playing music. If his interest in biology had waned, there were other avenues he could pursue. I assumed that he would eventually go to graduate school. This might have been unrealistic but how could I know? These hopes and dreams are now in the realm of lost possibilities.

Jon's life ended as a tragedy. The world was open to him but he was cheated of the life he might have had.

Then, almost twenty years elapsed. Martha got married and had her three children and Mark's career evolved into something so special that none of us could have either imagined or anticipated. The next chapters describe Mark, our oldest son and first-born child, what his early years were like, how he died, and how we were all impacted by his untimely death.

MARK, OUR FIRST SON

M ARK, our first child, was a most wanted and cherished baby. His story is that of a happy, out-going, playful and smart little boy who became a rebellious teen-ager and eventually a talented, innovative, and famous musician of his generation. It is also an account of the way he challenged not only himself, but also his family. Finally, it is a story of a remarkable turnaround and a great loss.

Mark was born early in the morning of September 24, 1952. Since at that time, fathers were not allowed in the labor and delivery area, Bob kissed me good-bye, and the door closed behind me. The doctor told Bob "you might as well go home and get some sleep since a first baby can take quite a while." Bob did, but probably felt guilty since the baby arrived quickly and he was not there.

Because I was given scopolamine during delivery, I remembered nothing about the birth and did not even know if I'd had the baby. When I awoke, I asked "What did I have?" "You had a lovely boy." "I want to see him." "You will once you get back to your room. He's in the nursery." When I got to my room, I was eager to see and hold my baby. At the same time, I felt cheated out of the experience. Then I overheard the nurse in the hall ask "where's the Sandman baby?" and heard the reply "there's no Sandman baby here." I panicked, but fortunately the lost baby had been sent to the wrong floor. Once he was found, they brought him to me.

I was very proud of our perfect little boy. It was a time, however, that I longed for my mother. She died of liver cancer when I was fourteen. Since I was an only child, she and I were close, and her death left a terrible void in my life. I wanted to share this joy with her, woman to woman. She would have been so happy to have her own grandson. However, both of our existing families were delighted and Bob and I marveled that producing someone we wanted could give so much pleasure to our families.

The next issue was the *brit*, (circumcision). In those days, for maternity, you stayed in the hospital at least five to seven days. Since the idea of a circumcision did not appeal to me anyway, I preferred to have it done in the hospital. Bob arranged for a pediatrician, who was also a *mohel* (i.e. a person qualified to perform the ritual), do the procedure in the circumcision room at the Beth Israel Hospital. The whole family came but I stayed and fretted in my hospital room. I thought the procedure barbaric and did not care if it was an important tradition or even if it was more hygienic. After what seemed like an eternity, the nurse brought the baby back to me. He was tired and hungry, so he suckled contentedly. I soon felt better and we went home later that day.

We ran afoul with the baby's name. For some reason, I had been certain he would be a girl and had barely thought of a boy's name. Therefore, when the baby was clearly a boy, we had to do some quick thinking. We knew what his Hebrew name would be, since he was still to be named after my mother, whose Hebrew name was *Chaya*, meaning life, but we had more trouble with his English name. We had looked through books of names and liked Mark. We also liked Christopher thinking the name meant disciple of God and also that it would resemble his Hebrew name, *Chiam*. When we sent out birth announcements, we got a swift reaction from our relatives. Apparently in the Jewish tradition, there are a few names you really cannot use such as Christine or Christopher. We were embarrassed and sheepishly renamed him Mark Jeffrey, sent out new announcements, and changed his birth certificate.

Because I was superstitious, we had no furniture for the baby when we got home. Therefore we lined a laundry basket with blankets and put Mark in it. The first few nights he slept noisily in our room. None of us got much sleep as I either had to check on him or feed him all night long. While I was in the hospital, Goldie had purchased a layette. My father gave us a white crib, baby dresser and bathinette, (an old fashioned plastic bathing arrangement on a wooden frame) which we had requested beforehand. Thus, within a day or two we had everything organized. The furniture filled the little room and in a tiny alcove, we had a rocking chair. There wasn't an inch of space for anything else but it was a nice, cozy little nesting place.

I felt euphoric in those early days although Mark neither slept well nor was easily comforted. It was close to six months before he slept through the night so, like every new mother, I suffered from chronic fatigue. It seemed to me he was hungry all the time yet vomited a lot. I worried that he was not getting enough to eat. Before long, however, he gained weight and became a chubby, healthy, active baby.

Mark had blonde curly hair, big blue eyes and an affectionate nature. He loved to be read to, to do puzzles, to listen to music. When he was six months old, however, I learned that I was pregnant again. Although we were happy to be having another baby, I always felt that we deprived Mark of some of his babyhood.

Still, his first year was exciting. He walked early (nine months), climbed over the sides of his crib and onto kitchen counters, and was busy and active all the time. It was clear that he was taking in a lot of information and knew what was being said, but he did not talk, except for a few words, until he was close to three. Even then, when he was in nursery school, he said nothing in school. Once at home, he would tell me page- by- page what was in the books that had been read to him. Except for his first few words, i.e. "bokki" for bottle and "bankie" for blanket, he spoke clearly and in sentences when he began to talk.

Because he was so active, he was hard to contain. When he was about fourteen months old, and I was very pregnant with Martha, I bundled him in his light blue snowsuit and put him in the play yard Bob had built for him so he could play outside. The next thing I knew, he was at our back door with a big grin. I was aghast. "Mark, how did you get here?" Since he wasn't speaking, he just smiled. "Show me how you got over the fence." We went back into the yard and I put him in the play yard. Within a few minutes, he had pulled his little red wagon to the fence and easily climbed over it, looking very proud of himself.

* * *

A few weeks later, the night before Martha was born, Bob and I were watching a program on our first and newly purchased television set. While Mark was happily playing with my keys, I was stretched out on the sofa and thought I had my eye on him, but when it was time to put him to bed, I realized that he no longer had my keys. "Where are the keys?" I asked. He smiled. We searched and searched but failed to find them. I was irritated, but what could I do? I couldn't make him tell me. In the middle of that night, I went to the hospital to have Martha. Afterward, our household became very busy and we replaced the keys. Six months later I was getting ready for a dinner party and looked for a tablecloth in a dining room drawer. Lo and behold, there in the corner were my keys! Apparently the drawer was ajar and Mark had dropped them in.

Early on, Mark used drawings to express his emotions. When he was in pre-school, he brought home a drawing that consisted of black cubic blocks. "Is there a story to this picture?" I asked. "That's my school and it's burned down", he said. It happened to be a time when he did not like his teacher or the school. Another time, when he was in kindergarten, he brought home a picture of a train engineer. He proudly said "This is my Daddy, an engineer." "Mark, you know Daddy's not that kind of engineer." "I know" he said, "but this is really more interesting."

When Mark started school, he did not know his letters and didn't seem to care. In kindergarten, his teacher assured us he would be a good reader. She was right because by Christmas of first grade he was reading well. In second grade, he'd invite friends over to read. He and his friend would read sitting on opposite ends of the couch, quietly absorbed in their books. It seemed to me to be a strange way to socialize, but Mark was perfectly happy. He remained an omnivorous reader throughout his life.

Mark never saw things the way the rest of us did. The fact that he was a maverick in the family made family dynamics hard for him. It was also difficult for him to be the only child with brown hair. All the other children and I had red hair. Even our dachshunds had reddish hair. This shouldn't have been a big issue, but often when we'd go out, people would say "Oh, look at all the red heads" and then turn to Mark and say "Are you part of the family too?" Of course, he was part of the family. At one time he said to me, "Mommy, why don't you color your hair brown? I know it can be done, I've seen it on TV. Then you'd look more like me." We talked about his hair being very nice and just like Daddy's, but that didn't seem to help. He simply felt different and didn't like it.

When Mark was in fifth grade, he played trombone in the all - city orchestra. One day I got a call from the director who complained that Mark was poking the kids in front of him with his slide. He said "We can't have such behavior and if he doesn't stop, he'll have to leave." When I asked Mark to explain, he said "Gee, Mom, what do you expect me to do when I have eighty-five measures rest? It's so boring!" I could not dispute that, but presented the alternatives to him. He chose to behave better and stay in the orchestra. Actually when he played his trombone at home and the windows were open, the younger kids in the neighborhood would listen, and then say with a shrug, "Well, there's Mark playing his trombonie!" All the younger kids in the neighborhood knew and liked Mark and thought his loud instrument was special.

Music for Mark started early as we went to a lot of concerts and of course, listened to records. Some of the music was just silly and fun, but some was serious. When he began to study, he was a quick learner, but did not necessarily stick with things when they became more difficult. He began with recorder lessons, played the piano, and finally trombone.

Mark had formal training. Guitar came later. He also sang and was in the first Troubadours, an elite middle school honors chorus. He looked and felt very special in his white shirt, black tie, black pants and gold V-neck sweater with the Troubadour insignia on it. In addition, he liked being part of this chorus, even though there were only a few boys. It seems surprising and rather special to me that Martha now conducts the same group for the city of Newton.

* * *

All was not rosy for him in school, however. He frustrated his teachers. If something interested him, he learned quickly and would excel; if it didn't, he would turn to something else. This was especially true in math. In retrospect, he probably had a learning disability in math, but at that time, such problems were not diagnosed.

By middle school, we thought a private school with smaller classes would let him get the attention and supervision he needed. Mark balked at this. "I'm not leaving my friends. I won't go! I'm fine. I'll work hard in junior high." Unfortunately, we did not press him. Thus, in public school, in some areas, – English, social studies, music, he did exceptionally well. He even learned German quickly, but then began to act up in class. His teacher put the disrupters out into the hall, which he called "Siberia". Mark was "King of Siberia". Actually, he remembered a lot of German, which he used in his later years.

In September of eighth grade, Mark had his Bar Mitzvah. We had changed temples a year or so earlier and although I doubted he knew enough, in fact, he did. He learned language easily and well. In preparing for the big event, Mark learned he was supposed to wear a real suit. I decided Bob should be in charge of this part of the preparations – a father-son thing, so Bob, never a shopper, dutifully took Mark on this expedition. Both came back long-faced and disenchanted. The suit they bought was a simple gray flannel, entirely appropriate, but Mark balked.

"I won't wear this suit. The pants are too baggy. Pants should fit like my blue jeans. Look at this jacket. It's not cut right. It looks terrible. Nobody wears this kind of thing." We forced him to wear the suit after many more quarrels. Later we learned we could have rented a suit and saved him and us a lot of grief. Now khakis and a sport jacket are usually what are worn.

The Bar Mitzvah itself surprised me. I had gone to very few, never had any religious training and had few expectations about the event. When I saw Mark on the *bima* (dais), with his two grandfathers, and saw the Torah passed down from generation to generation, I felt as if our Jewish family had a heritage that had been going on for thousands of years. Mark's Bar Mitzvah seemed indeed a special rite of passage into our tradition and the beginning of adulthood. I was glad to be a part of it. Mark did very well and made us proud. He enjoyed all the praise and presents he received.

Around that time, he really wanted straight hair that he could flip back with a toss of his head instead of the kinky, curly hair that he had. So for his fourteenth birthday, we had his hair straightened. He was elated and even seemed to take more interest in his appearance. After going back for several hair straightening treatments, he got tired of the procedure and stopped. By that time he began to let his hair grow wildly.

By tenth grade, some real problems arose. As the academics became more demanding, Mark's performance became more erratic. His English studies were fine, but every other subject began to deteriorate. His grades plummeted. Also, his friends, who were high achievers, became less interested in him, and he began to choose friends who skipped school, and were not involved in their studies. Certainly, they seemed to have less supervision.

Furthermore, it appeared to us that he cared less and less about how he looked – he became sloppy, dirty, and indifferent, like his new friends, whom he rarely brought home. His manners and language became deplorable, lots of four letter words and poor grammar. He dropped his programs in music, sports and his studies. We did not know what he was doing, and he was not telling us.

I had always been a straight shooter, eager to please and do the right things. Whatever adolescent rebellion I felt was understated and not acted out. Proper manners had been instilled in me early on, and I had tried to teach them to our children. It felt like Mark was flouting my standards and me, and this led to many arguments. Although I tried to focus on his strengths, I simply did not understand his disregard for what we considered important. In retrospect I can see that in his eyes we were being rigid and controlling.

We certainly tried to control his appearance. To me, his disheveled clothes and wild hair represented the disintegration that seemed to be going on internally. Mark became moody, belligerent, disrespectful and unreliable.

There was a lot we were unwilling to see or acknowledge. There were terrible arguments. When we said in desperation,

"Mark, you have such potential! You're so good looking and smart and loved. You can be anything you want, and we want to help you. You really are lucky. Why are you throwing it all away?"

His reply was "Your idea of doing anything I want is if I'm a doctor or lawyer or executive or engineer. You only want me to be a professional of some kind, not just an ordinary person."

We were stunned, and said "Yes, we want you to be productive, but the choice really is yours. We just want you to try to make the most of your gifts. And we want you to be happy and independent and healthy and responsible."

When I look back on these scenes now, I realize that we should have been more empathic. At the time, we did not understand and were not tuned into his issues. He shared few of his thoughts but, I'm sure now, he wanted to be heard. At that time, we were so bewildered and worried about the direction his life seemed to be taking that we did not ask or even listen. If I had it to do over, I would have listened to him more and tried harder to understand his conflicts. Unfortunately we can't undo what was done.

Mark's high school career became disastrous. We had nasty arguments about homework and almost everything else. Bob and I tried to choose our battles but it became more and more difficult to find neutral issues. Then after slamming the door to his room so much that the door became lopsided, he decided he needed more privacy and wanted his own pad away from the family. Since we had an extra large room in the basement, we said he could have it and decorate it to his satisfaction. We weren't prepared for the psychedelic paints he sprayed on the walls, or for the mess he made, we but let him have his own space where he and his friends could go. That helped for a while.

Bob remembered finding Mark asleep sitting in a chair in the basement after he supposedly was taking his final exams in his junior year. Apparently, Mark had sneaked out of the house through a broken window in the basement and had come back the same way. We really did not know what to make of this and, with disbelief, did not want to face the reality of the situation.

A few weeks later, he brought home a dreadful report card. He and I were standing at the foot of our stairs, the report card in front of me when I confronted him.

"How can this be? You'd have to work at it to get grades that are failing in almost all subjects. Where have you been? You leave the house every day to go to school. You'd do better than this just sitting in class!"

"Oh, there's a reason", he replied. "I didn't go to my classes, didn't write my papers, do any work!"

How could he have gotten away with this? Why hadn't the school contacted us? Why did things have to come to this point? What were we going to do now? Would he even graduate high school? How could this have happened to our first born, the child we loved and had such high hopes for? What did we do that was so bad? We were angry, felt sorry for ourselves and frightened about what might lie ahead for Mark.

We didn't know that some of our friends had seen him lolling about in Newton Center during school hours, but never mentioned it to us. We were infuriated that we had never heard from the school. Usually, if a child were absent we'd get a call asking if he was sick, but we received no calls at all. It became clear that something had to be done. Although he denied it, we think he was doing drugs at that time. He certainly was smoking cigarettes and probably marijuana. We did not know about the marijuana, but we fussed and fumed about the cigarettes.

We knew something drastic had to be done. Mark had taken his SAT's and done well. He also had a very high IQ. These were in his favor. Bob began taking Mark to visit boarding schools. Because of his potential indicated by these tests, schools were interested in him, but only if he would cut his hair. Mark was adamant; he absolutely would not. Even we became annoyed not only with Mark, but with the schools, for by that time we thought his hair was not the major problem. Ironically, only a few years later, hair would really be a non-issue even at these schools. But it was a big issue then. Finally a small alternative school, Pembroke Place, accepted him and he agreed to go. We were both relieved and sad. Though we preferred to have him under our roof and part of the family, he was so disruptive, and caused so much turmoil and anguish we felt the family needed a break from him. I'm quite sure he felt the same need to get out of our household. He was probably as relieved as we were.

During that time, we continued to worry about Mark and his future. At first it seemed that sending him to boarding school was a good move. We had devoted so much time and energy to dealing with him that we felt we were neglecting our other children. With Mark away, our household was much more peaceful and the younger children were getting more attention. Mark would occasionally write or call home and report that all was well. Once however, he came home with a presentable haircut. We presumed then that he had gotten into trouble of some sort and that the haircut was the mandated punishment. We asked Mark if that were so. He just said "Don't worry. It's all taken care of."

Another time, we were riding on route 128 at night and I said to Bob "I think I just saw Mark thumbing a ride". "How could that be?" asked Bob. We turned around and retraced our route, and sure enough, there was Mark. I was so furious and frightened, I was afraid to say much. Mark got into the car looking embarrassed. He was silent. We had been going to see our family therapist. On this night, since Mark was a captive, we took him with us. Mark sat there, uncommunicative. Our therapist suggested we take Mark back to his school, and let the school deal with the problems. We did. When we called the school the next day, we were told that everything was under control. They were not very communicative either.

Mark finally graduated. He had made friends there, but most of the boys had had problems of one sort or another. But so, of course, did Mark. My father, uncle, Goldie and all the other children went to the graduation. Only a few of the graduates were going on to college and fortunately Mark was one of them. He was accepted by Windham College, in Vermont. Before he went there, he went on an Outward Bound program in Vail, Colorado. We had hoped this would be a positive, insightful adventure for him and we were glad that he seemed eager to go.

Mark was overwhelmed by the experience. It was quite rigorous. In one of his few letters at that time he related:

> "This is the routine. We get up between 4:30 and 6:00 AM and we hit the trail within two hours of that. An average hiking day is 8-9 hours or 6-10 miles. There are nine people including me in my patrol and one leader. We sleep three under a plastic sheet which we tie to trees and our ice axes. We carry 4-5 days dry rations at a time, with fresh food re-supplies, mail and store in between."

He continued:

> "– on the 9th mile of a 10 mile hike from Upper Cataract Lake (11,000 ft) to Piney River a kid in my patrol fell and broke his leg, so now we are 8. He was taken out by helicopter after a 5 ½ hour wait in a swampy area. Just like Viet Nam."

The most challenging ordeal included leaving him alone in the mountains for a few days when he had to fend and forage for himself. Basically, he felt it was a good experience and made him see things in himself. Although we were glad to hear from him and enjoyed his letters, we worried about how he would cope and stay safe. We were hopeful that this experience had helped him and would be a turning point. Mark did not share his feelings.

That fall at Windham initially went well. By the middle of the year, however, Mark flunked out. Eventually, we learned that in order to earn some extra money, Mark allegedly was writing papers for others, and neglecting his own.

When he came home again we said he either had to go to school of some kind or go to work full time. Otherwise he could not live at home. That was the TOUGH LOVE recommended by our family therapist. Mark opted to work for Bob, undoubtedly not a good choice for he worked only a few days. We repeated our conditions. He didn't believe us. He stayed out one night and then came back with a friend in time for dinner the next night. We fed them, but reiterated our terms for his living at home. He was shocked, but said he understood. He went to his "pad", picked up a few things, took some food, and left with his friend in a January snow storm.

What to do now? I wept both from anger at Mark for putting us through this and because I couldn't believe what we'd done. The other children were aghast and frightened. Had we done the right thing?

Mark did not contact us for about a month. Meanwhile, my fantasies were running wild. I imagined him freezing on a sidewalk or holed up in some dreadful place. We just didn't know. When Mark finally called us, he reported that he was living in a group house in Vermont, feeling fine and doing odd jobs. He also said he was getting food stamps. We were glad to hear from him, and to learn that he was safe and apparently not in trouble. We also invited him to come home for our Passover Seder. Much to our surprise and pleasure, he came. He was dirty and disheveled, but we were glad to have him home. Years later he said "kicking me out" was the best thing we could have done for him, although he didn't think so at the time. We were relieved that he could understand why we had done what we did.

From that time, Mark's real adventures began. Yet he always seemed to resurface and want to be part of the family. I don't recall the exact sequence of his escapades, but I remember one whole winter he lived in an abandoned miner's cabin near Breckenridge, Colorado. I doubt that he bathed all the time he was there and have no idea what he ate. We could only communicate with him through the Gold Nugget Saloon, where he apparently went for some libation and socialization. If he was not there when we called, he eventually got the message and reversed the charges to call us back.

About 1972, he lived in the Northwest. When the rest of us went to Vancouver, British Columbia, where Bob was involved in a conference, we invited Mark to join us. At that time, he was working as a cook on a fishing boat. We arranged to meet him at the ferry from Seattle to Vancouver. At the dock, Bob, Martha, Jon, Roger and I stood waiting and waiting as everyone disembarked. Where was Mark? After a very long time, when we thought our communications must have gone awry, Mark finally emerged, the last to get off the ferry. The customs officers had thoroughly searched this long-haired, messy, dirty, unshaven, suspicious looking young man and his knapsack, and eventually released him. Mark thought it was funny; we thought it was humiliating. He went with us to our rather posh hotel, had a meal with us, spent the night, showered, and had breakfast. The rest of us were going on a train trip to Banff and Lake Louise, but Mark chose to go back to Seattle. It was a heart-wrenching good-bye for us all as he returned on the ferry and we took the train.

Following that experience, Mark continued to do things that baffled us. He did many exotic things. In June 1974, again from the Northwest, he wrote:

> "I finally got myself the job I've been looking for. It's a 52 foot salmon fishing trawler and tuna jigboat *(abalone) and we'll be fishing the west coast from Washington and Oregon for salmon (coho or silvers) until July and then all the way from Mexico to Canada for the tuna. The guy I work for is a high liner which means one of the top fishermen. He's a real nice guy and it's a good solid boat, built in 1948. – Jim has a lot to teach me and I'll make real good money too. – I'm getting the feel of the ocean, getting my sea legs – I cook and clean, take the wheel, watch the gear and generally do everything he tells me to and we've been getting along pretty well. I work from dawn to dusk."

We were proud of his independence and adventurous spirit.

While in the Northwest, he wrote to Martha from a small town on the Olympic Peninsula:

> "I'm working in a cannery here – as a crane operator, and then hopefully will be getting on one of the company owned boats – It's very beautiful here right now, although a little rainy, and in the summer should be just outrageous. The Olympic National Rain Forest begins just north of here, with 10-foot ferns, huge sweet smelling cedar trees and giant piles of moss everywhere. It seems very magical walking through the woods there, and it seems like you can see little leprechauns and hobbits darting behind trees if you turn around fast enough."

When I found this letter, I appreciated his descriptions, but the best part for us was to see that he was in touch with his sister.

He moved from Washington to Alaska where he worked on a crab tender until he developed an allergy to crabs. He had hoped to make a lot of money; instead, because of the high cost of living, he barely made enough to make ends meet.

Subsequently he went to Central and South America where he roamed, lost his passport climbing Machu Picchu, and then ended in Brazil where he lived for six months. It was in Brazil that Mark began to play music more earnestly, learned to speak Portuguese and became aware of some of the political repression there. He wrote:

"Here there is total censorship. When we did our concert in Niteroi, across the bay, Flavio (the band leader) first had to file all the lyrics to the show to be approved and send in the union card of everyone playing. They (the government) – refused some songs for strange reasons, – references to war, poverty, current events, – poetic imagery of fleeing across a borderline from one love to another was censored for implying a dissatisfaction with Brazil. Plays and movies are likewise edited. So are newspapers and organizations."

He sent us a clipping from a newspaper featuring him in a night club playing keyboard as well as guitar. In Brazil, he became quite ill with a serious infection that caused him to come home and from which he fortunately recovered. All of this time, he kept in touch with us, but was living a life we had difficulty understanding and knew little about. We feared for his safety, but were also concerned that life was passing him by. Where would his future lie? Now I wish we had appreciated his sense of adventure and desire for new and unusual experiences. But at the time we were short-sighted and apprehensive.

After Mark returned home and got the medications he needed, he found an apartment in Cambridge. Then he started studying music and playing guitar more seriously. He did odd jobs to support himself. Although we wanted to help him, we felt any money we gave him would be used for things that were harmful to him. We tried to be generous for special gifts but it was always a dilemma for us. We were quite sure that his grandmother, Goldie, was giving him money against our wishes, but we were not involved and nobody told us.

Intermittently he would take off with his friends, most of whom we did not know. We rarely even knew where he was and certainly did not know what he was doing. At one time, I received a call: "Hi, Mom. I'm in a bit of trouble. I got picked up by the police in Texas and am in jail.

I can only make one call. Can you arrange for me to get bail?" He sounded frightened. It was not hard to imagine my reaction. I was terrified and wavered between panic, anger, worry and fear. Now what?

Immediately, I consulted Bob. We arranged bail and contacted relatives in Dallas to help us out. We asked our neighbor and friend, Bob Griesse, what we should do. Bob was a minister who had had experience with kids in trouble. He said he had a colleague in Texas and would contact him about getting a lawyer. It turned out that the car Mark and his friends were in had been stopped and then searched. Mark had a small amount of marijuana in his pocket, and that was enough to put him in jail in Texas. It was considered a felony, which Mark understood. He admitted he was scared. Fortunately, everything got worked out. After one night Mark was free on bail and stayed with some of our Texas relatives in Dallas. The lawyer recommended by Bob Griesse's friend took the case and Mark was miraculously cleared. It was not an experience any of us had ever imagined could happen to someone in our family. How could Mark, who was about twenty at the time, do this to himself and to us? What a way to impose on the good will of our relatives, who were amazingly tolerant and helpful! We were ashamed, embarrassed, worried and furious at Mark. It certainly was something we would not want to go through again.

It was not too long after that that Mark came home with a pack on his back. Bob was running for School Committee in Newton at the time and Mark not only wanted to vote for his father, but wanted to work for him at the polls. We were delighted to see him dressed in his blue jeans and a flannel shirt. He got cleaned up and then asked winsomely if we thought he'd be a hindrance or a help. We assured him it was wonderful for him to come home, and in fact he stood at the polls and then at City Hall when the election returns came in. When Bob lost by a small margin, I felt really sad. Mark came over, put his arm around me and said: "I'm proud of Dad. He put up a good fight!" I replied "It means a lot to have you here! I'm glad you came home."

When Mark was twenty-five, he came back to Cambridge and said he was ready to go back to college. "I want to be a 'Renaissance Man.'" He was living in an apartment and still playing his guitar with pick-up groups. His plan was to attend U. Mass and support himself by driving a cab in Boston. We agreed to pay his tuition and give him a stipend to supplement his living expenses. This began a whole new phase of his life. He worked diligently, and I think, felt good about himself. Finally he had a life style we could understand and appreciate.

He seemed to take pride in being a cab driver and even later wrote a song "Supersex" where the words "Taxi, Taxi" rang out. At the time, however, we worried about him. His hours were long and often through the night. One afternoon, Bob and I were driving in Boston and a taxi honked at us. It was Mark, grinning broadly and waving to us, with a fare in the back seat. We were delighted that he seemed glad to see us and waved back enthusiastically.

Before long, however, we got a call that Mark was in the ICU at Carney Hospital. It was a sunny Sunday afternoon. Mark was in Dorchester and had picked up two teenagers. He later admitted that he knew better, but thought on a Sunday afternoon there would be no problem. He obviously was wrong. One of the kids attacked him, stabbed him in the chest with a knife, took Mark's eight dollars, pulled out the knife and fled. Mark had the presence of mind to radio the cab company who arranged for him to be taken to the hospital. The puncture collapsed his lung, but fortunately missed his heart. It was a painful experience in many ways for him and frightening for us as well. After about a week in the ICU, he was discharged and directly returned to his classes. He seemed to heal properly without further complications. I don't think he drove a cab after that.

That was not the end of the story, however. Two years to the day, (I remember, because it was my birthday both times), Mark was house sitting for his grandmother. We got a call from him. "I've got a terrible belly ache. I've had it a few days but it's getting worse. I don't know what to do. I need help! I'm in terrible pain." Bob called our friend, Dr. Ben Selling, who actually came to the house to examine him and immediately said: "Mark needs to go to the hospital right now. I think he needs surgery." Apparently, the knife wound had left a hole in Mark's diaphragm. Mark had eaten a heavy dinner and some of the food had gone through the hole. It needed to be repaired stat. We took him to the hospital where he had preliminary diagnostic tests. Then Dr. Selling found a surgeon who repaired the problem. It was a terrible experience for Mark.

He came back to his old upstairs room at our house to recuperate. It was a dreadful time for us as well. Jonny, with whom Mark had recently become good friends, had died only eight weeks before and that was only sixteen months after Roger's death. It felt unreal. Bob and I were emotionally drained and now with Mark's need for life saving emergency surgery we wondered how many times we could be taken to the post. We felt fragile and vulnerable. Before this latest crisis, we had made plans to go to Club Med in the Bahamas for a week to have a mindless time and try to pull ourselves together. Since a friend, M.J. Henderson, a nurse, was living with us at that time, she assured us she could and would manage Mark's care. By then, because he was recovering and we were totally depleted, we went. I have subsequently felt guilty when I think of our going away at that time, since our place as parents should have been with him. We just felt empty; we had nothing to give.

Again Mark went back to U. Mass, – some of the time in Amherst, some of the time in Boston. He said he preferred Boston, however, because the student body was more mature and interesting. During his hospitalization, his girl friend from U. Mass., Toni, called looking for him. She was stunned to learn that he was in the hospital and said she'd contact him. A few months later, Mark brought Toni to Martha and Ted's wedding. She was attractive with long brown hair. She wore a sophisticated sleeveless black dress and seemed at ease as she introduced herself to the other wedding guests, none of whom she knew. We were impressed with her savoir faire and felt comfortable with her. She was spirited, bright, talkative and appealing. She clearly liked Mark, and we enjoyed her.

Mark graduated from U. Mass. in 1981 at the age of twenty-nine. He had majored in political science and Portuguese. He even spent a summer term at the University of Lisbon to study Portuguese. While there, he wrote that he had "three hours of school a day" and that he was "streamlining (his) tongue on this new brand of Portuguese (i.e. not Brazilian) and eating well". I think he took every course offered in that language at U. Mass. He did extremely well. He had been offered an internship to work in international trade, but turned it down. After his graduation with honors, he announced: "I did it for you, Mom, and now I want to be a rock musician!" And so the next era began.

Mark 1965

Fisherman Mark in the Northwest

Martha and Mark January 1982

Mark's Career Unfolds

W̲E were astounded although should not have been. People often ask where Mark's and Martha's music and creative abilities came from. Well, music in both Bob's family and mine has had a prominent role. My mother was a fine pianist who played classical music and often accompanied solo players. However, she could also play "by ear" and would come home after a musical, sit down at the piano and play what she had just heard. In addition, Bob's father was a cellist who played in amateur string groups in Boston, but who also sought string ensembles to join as he traveled around the world.

Music was important to me as a child. I played piano, violin and even the saxophone. Then after we had children, I took up recorder and played in many consorts. There was no question about our children having to learn an instrument, except for Roger who truly was not able. We felt it was not only a good discipline, but also the best way to learn to appreciate music. I remember when Mark was eight and we went to a chamber music concert. At that time he had started to play recorder and piano. He sat very quietly throughout the concert and then announced that he liked this concert better than listening to a big orchestra since he could see and hear each instrument. As he got older, even though he continued to enjoy different kinds of music, he certainly preferred his own style.

Mark's paternal grandmother and aunt were and are well-known artists and Mark too, did a lot of drawings, sketches and photographs that were exhibited. I think these influences, in addition to his interest in innovative cooking, all contributed to his creative bent.

Because my own training was classical and disciplined in a different way, it was hard for me to understand what Mark was doing. His was not the music of my generation. Since we were very proud of his academic achievements, we had hoped that he would begin to pursue a different career and continue his music as an avocation. We were dismayed that he had chosen music as his path and were not supportive. Do I now feel guilty about this? You bet. But at the time, we were very disappointed and worried. Being a rock musician is a hard, unpredictable, insecure life.

About the time Mark graduated college, he moved into Toni's apartment. Toni had confidence in him. She felt he was special even though he tended to be messy and self-centered. We were grateful that they were together and thought she was very good for him. During that time, he played in various bands and did catering, often with Toni, to support himself.

In the 1980's, Mark joined David Champagne to start a new band, *Treat Her Right.* They played together with two others for a few years and between 1988 and 1990 they produced three albums, *Treat Her Right, Tied to the Tracks* and *What's Good for You.* The band was quite popular but eventually they broke up. While Mark worked hard, he refused to play music that was not his own. Therefore he gave up opportunities to earn money playing for weddings and Bar Mitzvahs because he took his music seriously and thought it would be demeaning to play popular music just to earn money.

We often wondered how he supported himself in those early musical years, since much of the time when the band got gigs they played for beer money and the chance for some exposure. RCA produced one album for them and that certainly helped, but our assumption was that Toni and Goldie helped him both financially and emotionally. We later heard that other family members helped out. However, Mark never talked to us about his financial affairs; nor did he ask us for money. About all we did for him was pay for his medical insurance. We feel sad that he was not comfortable enough to approach us, for I'm quite sure we would have helped. I regret now that we were not closer and more understanding and supportive.

Eventually Mark and Toni split up. They had been together eleven and a half years. We felt sad about this. We loved Toni who by this time had become part of the family. It seemed to us that they were both discombobulated by the separation. Toni was more communicative with us than Mark. She was hurt, angry and bitter. Rightfully, she felt that she had given up many years to be with him and had supported and had faith in him, when we certainly did not.

No one ever said he was easy to be with, but he was bright, funny, witty and affectionate. Even with us, he always had a big grin, a hug and kiss when he came to visit. And he did seem to have a sense of family, of wanting to belong, of wanting to make us proud.

After they broke up, Toni helped Mark find an apartment and a room-mate. The apartment was in a loft in an industrial building in Cambridge, but he made his half of their space a studio and bedroom and seemed happy when we came to visit. For one holiday, he invited the whole family to come for a party. To get to his place, we had to go up in a freight elevator. Once in his apartment, we were in a bachelor pad, which was full of mismatched furniture, odds and ends of dishes, cigarette butts, a collection of guitars mounted on the walls, and lots of musical equipment filling the space. Mark wanted to make it a party and prepared the whole meal. He served us with his collection of miscellaneous dishes and glassware and made little of the fact that his lifestyle was far from the way he was brought up. He was glad to entertain all of us in his apartment; it was fun for us, too. Furthermore, Martha's boys, his nephews, were intrigued with all the instruments and gadgets and loved the whole experience.

Actually, having had an ordinary, rather privileged, family life in Newton embarrassed Mark. He felt that was not the picture he wanted to present. Considering the life style he had chosen this was understandable. What could be more prosaic than coming from a stable family who had lived for many years in one house? And from his perspective, having a father who was an engineer and a mother who was a social worker did not enhance his image. My sense is that it would have been more interesting for him if we had been more dysfunctional than we were so that his background was not so plain.

* * *

We did not even go to many of his concerts. He often invited us to his gigs and when we appeared he was delighted and cordial but it was awkward for us. Partly, we felt like fish out of water at his events. The milieu was smoky, the music was loud; the young people were really into the beat and we were not. In addition, we found it difficult to go to performances that often started after eleven at night. Frequently, they were during the week and we had to get up early the next morning to go to work. Mark also resented our going to Martha's concerts. However, hers were eight o'clock on week-ends or the concerts her children gave were even earlier, so it was more manageable. Even though he did not go to her performances, he was offended that Martha and Ted went to very few of his. Nevertheless, when we went to see him perform, he was aware that we were not comfortable and tried to make us feel welcome. Now I'm sorry that we did not make more of an effort to attend. We should have. There are so many "should haves"!

Mark's aunt and uncle, Jo and Bob Asher, went to lots of his gigs, as did many of his young cousins in the area. Actually, wherever Mark traveled around the country, he invited relatives to come to his performances and would get them complimentary tickets. We received some funny telephone calls from cousins our age who attended some of his gigs in bars they would not have ordinarily been seen in. They laughed and chalked it up to a new experience. Mark delighted in their being there and their support. Furthermore, the younger relatives really understood and liked his music.

There were a few times Mark performed during the day. Then all of us went, i.e. Bob and I, Martha, Ted and the children, and we were treated royally. Joseph Sater, the proprietor of the Middle East where the band played was very fond of Mark and extremely cordial to us. While outside there was a long line waiting to enter, our party was ushered in immediately and given a table. Mr. Sater brought snacks and juice to the children and drinks for us. We all remember those times fondly.

At any rate, his life and career went on. In 1989, Mark, Bill Conway and Dana Colley teamed up to become the *Morphine* rock band. I know we were dismayed by their name. What did it say about Mark? What was he trying to convey? When we asked him he said "Well, Morpheus was the God of Sleep and Sandman, my name, implies sleeping so it felt like an appropriate name." That was hard for us to accept. Morphine in our minds was a drug and what image was he trying to project? His nephews and niece could not even wear his T shirts with the name *Morphine* to school. Recently the *Boston Phoenix* newspaper (October 17, 2006), said that the Plough and Stars Bar where *Morphine* was performing had said that "they had to play under a different name, 'Prophecy 3', because the owners of the Plough weren't so sure about having the name '*Morphine*' on their chalk board." We, too, were embarrassed by their name. For a long time we had trouble even saying the name of his group. After a while, however, it became easier. It was just a name for a rock band.

Eventually *Morphine* became internationally successful. The music was called "low rock" and most of it had a noir quality to it. Mark played his two stringed non-fretted slide bass, which became his trademark. Still, there were some fun, lilting songs and some ballads, which I liked the best. Their success was hard for us to believe, and even harder for us to understand. We comprehended neither their music nor their appeal. It was so different from our expectations or even from our world. They toured colleges, they were written up in newspapers and magazines and after a while, they were famous world-wide. We were delighted, although baffled with their rising fame. Finally, they could stay in nicer hotels and take time to sight-see in some of the places in which they were playing – Germany, Japan, Scandinavia, France, England, Ireland, Italy, and even Tasmania.

When they performed in music festivals out of the country, we'd receive many postcards. For example: an excited note from Copenhagen "playing some huge festival – 80-150,000 people at one time", a note from Japan starting with "Greetings, honorable parents from Mark in Japan – finished our 5 city tour in Sendai tonite. It was great! – Saw a Buddhist Temple on our day off yesterday. Spiritually recharging. Off to France!" And from France "Everything is *très, très, très, bien* here in France. About 600 plus people at each show, but Paris next week is sold out for 1500! And a second show added there too!" And from Norway "Cold here! Only gets dusky for a couple of hours. Skol!" Everything seemed upbeat; he sounded happy. We were glad to hear about his successes.

During this time, Mark met Sabine, a beautiful, sensitive woman with whom he fell in love. We grew to love her too and she soon became part of our family. She helped Mark feel good about himself which pleased us.

Since I did not know anything about how they met, I asked Sabine if she could tell me about it. Sabine said that while they had known each other for some time, they did not date until 1993. She wrote:

> "He courted me for quite a while and was nearly at the
> point of giving up hope when I realized I had fallen in
> love with him. It was very old-fashioned. We had a few
> months together before I went off to graduate school in

New Hampshire and *Morphine* took off and he started touring in earnest, which was tough for such a new relationship, but he was so encouraging of my independence and I looked to him for inspiration since he was so passionate about what he did."

It was not until Thanksgiving, 1993, when we went to our cousin's house for our traditional feast that we first met her. Our hostess said:

"Mark is going to be here. Did you know he's bringing a friend?"

"Is this friend a woman?" I asked.

She replied "I don't know, but I think so."

We welcomed this news since Mark had seemed to be at loose ends after he and Toni separated.

A short time later, Mark entered with Sabine, a lovely young woman who dazzled us with her beauty. She had a Middle Eastern appearance with her long dark, almost black hair, dark brown observant eyes and thick eyebrows. Her elegant outfit consisted of black pants, jacket and boots and a pale blue shirt. I'm sure our noisy, exuberant family overwhelmed her. Mark seemed protective of her and kept his arm around her as we peppered her with questions.

As much as we were trying to welcome (and assess) her, she undoubtedly was appraising us. I tried not to stare at this new woman in Mark's life. She seemed bright, self-assured and attentive. I remember trying to be discrete and not to ask too many questions which my children always accused me of doing. However, she seemed to be comfortable with whatever I asked. At the same time, she was observing our family. How did we interact? Who were all these people? Were they all relatives? How was Mark with his parents? With his sister Martha and her husband Ted? With his niece and nephews? To join a large family gathering as a newcomer and an outsider has to be difficult.

In contrast to how dressed up everyone else was, Mark wore an ivory colored ski sweater which was a bit stained and had a few holes. He brought several bottles of good wine. In addition, Mark also brought a delicious squash dish with pineapple, nuts and spices. We knew he was a good cook, yet were impressed since he rarely contributed anything to these meals. On that day he seemed more talkative and animated than usual. I suppose this was because things were going well for him and he was eager to talk about his recent successes.

While Mark wanted to take center stage, Sabine was sedate and a little removed. We were all curious about her. How serious was this relationship? Unlike Mark, Sabine had impeccable manners both in the way she addressed people and at the table. She, Mark, Martha and Ted were conversing and laughing at one end of the long table and were engaged with each other, despite occasionally being interrupted by Martha's children who wanted attention. It was particularly good to see Mark so relaxed and happy. He had come alone to family gatherings for the past three years after breaking up with Toni and we wondered how his friendship with Sabine would evolve.

Before long, however, Sabine and Mark became a couple. We thought they had a good relationship. As we grew comfortable with each other, Sabine seemed more open and joined Mark at most of our family events. We were delighted.

When we met her, Sabine was pursuing a Master of Science degree in environmental science at Antioch New England Graduate School in New Hampshire. At the time, Mark clearly was intrigued with her and gave up some of his workaholic schedule to go with her on some of her out-door adventures which surprised even him. Sabine was a naturalist, ecologist and writer. Mark said "She makes the world come alive for me. She shows me ways of seeing the natural world I had not experienced nor thought about before." He clearly loved her.

When, after graduating, she went to the Radcliffe Summer Institute for an intensive six week publishing course, Sabine said "I was overwhelmed and could not have gotten through it without Mark's support." I was glad to hear this. It seemed to me this was a sign that he was finally becoming a more mature, compassionate adult.

Meanwhile, Mark's career took off. He traveled a great deal and was becoming a celebrity. Suddenly, he had money and Sabine showed him how to enjoy it. He was able to take some vacations with her. They went to the Southwest where she had friends and wanted to do some research and writing, and they also took a trip, a pure vacation, to Belize. From there he wrote "checking out this interesting little country from a jungle lodge with a thatched roof – I am so happy!" We, too, were glad that he and Sabine were enjoying their special holiday.

Basically, Sabine is an intellectual, thirteen years younger than Mark, and in my opinion, very different in style. While Mark didn't seem to care much about formalities of speech and dress, Sabine was suave, worldly, secure and formal. However, they had both been bright rebellious teenagers. Sabine said she did not want to conform, but unlike Mark she always did well in school because she was afraid not to please her father.

One day Mark made a telephone request. "May Sabine leave her motorcycle in your garage for the winter?" This was a surprise. Sabine is a motorcyclist? She is and kept her big bike, a BMW GS R1000, in our garage for several seasons since she didn't ride it in the winter. When I asked her why she rides, she answered "I love the excitement and the freedom of being on the road. When I first start out, it's scary, but then I get comfortable and exhilarated." While she rode in the city and on longer trips to one of her family's homes in Waterville Valley, New Hampshire and to Maine, she was prudent. She always wore appropriate protective gear, such as a helmet, leather jacket, gloves and boots, and avoided risks.

She wrote that she bought it in 1996 when she was living in New York and turned 30. She said:

> "I had coveted that particular model for a long time and just happened on it while walking to work one morning. When Mark came to visit, I took him to the garage where it was parked to show it off and there were many others there as well. He kept pointing to them and saying 'is that it? Finally they got to mine, which is the last one and he gasped 'My God, it's huge – did you have to get the biggest bike out there?' His reaction made me laugh at the time, but he was just concerned and he was very endearing."

Although Mark feared riding, he agreed to take lessons so that they could both join a group in South Africa. From there, they planned to ride their bikes to Mt. Kilimanjaro and then hike to the top to bring in the new century. If he did not like riding the bike, he could ride in the van with their gear and join the others when they stopped. He was enthusiastic about starting in South Africa and making the trip, but was not excited about riding the bike. They planned to go in a group. Of course none of this worked out for Mark because he never saw the millennium. He died in July, 1999.

Sabine remained with the group. She joined them as they made the trip and left tokens in Mark's memory on top of the mountain. There they literally watched the dawn of the new century. It pleased us that she was able to do this both for herself and Mark.

For a while after Sabine and Mark had been going together, Sabine moved to New York to take a job editing an MIT publication. The move gave her the opportunity to meet people and make contacts. Mark helped her find and renovate an apartment. Then, whenever he could, he visited her. Two years later, Sabine returned to Boston where she could free lance, write and be closer to Mark, since for most of their relationship they had lived in separate states.

In Cambridge, they started living together for the first time, and Mark arranged to rent the loft next to where he had been living. The entry was the same. You still had to park in the commercial lot, climb onto the loading dock, and go up in the same clattery caged elevator. But the new loft was spectacular. The space was brick walled, vast and open with huge windows that brought in much light. They had a large bedroom which they could close off. It contained a work place, shelves, desk and computer for Sabine. A long hallway lined with books, both Sabine's and Mark's ran between the bedroom and kitchen. They fixed up the galley kitchen where Sabine insisted on a new stove even though,, as she explained, "Mark didn't mind the ratty one that was here." They had a whole set of matching dishes and miscellaneous pots and pans for Mark to use, since he enjoyed cooking. Sabine placed interesting teapots, vases and bottles on display. There was an ancient bathroom with an old fashioned footed tub. Sabine had painted the walls red and decorated the space with pictures, curtains and rugs. What a change this was from Mark's other loft across the hall! I was excited to see this transformation and was grateful to Sabine and happy for them both.

The best part of their loft was the rest of the space. It was an enormous open area which they broke into various functional units, though it had no dividers. Mark had a whole wall for his tapes, computer equipment and desk with good lighting. In the middle of the room on a large red oriental carpet was Mark's prize item, his newly purchased grand piano. It took center stage. To one side was the practice and recording area. Here too was a wall of tapes. There were also many amplifiers, recording and mixing equipment, guitars, drums, keyboards and various other instruments Mark had collected.

At the opposite wall was a dining area, a black leather sofa and chairs, bright oriental carpets, colorful pillows and a large coffee table.

It was the first time Mark had lived in a nicely appointed environment and I was pleased for him. In fact, Mark chuckled as he saw my reaction. I was excited by his living space and glad that he had Sabine, who clearly put a woman's touch on the loft. She was accustomed to good quality so she was not going to put up with a lot of Mark's making do. This was her home too.

They began to make a life together. Sabine went to all his concerts when he was in the Boston area and seemed comfortable with his friends. She did not travel with the group when they performed overseas although sometimes she would meet him in Europe. Mainly, I think, she wanted to settle down and convinced Mark to want that too. With great excitement they found a house in Somerville to buy. It was a "fixer-upper", but they shared a vision of what they wanted and had hired an architect to design the space according to their specifications. Sabine knew what she wanted to do with the garden and was eager to get started. Mark mentioned that they were reconfiguring the space and thinking about a fence to give them some privacy. They anticipated a great future. Mark was nervous, but also ecstatic about buying a house and seemed delighted with himself and what he and Sabine planned to do together. We never saw it.

According to Sabine, when they bought the house, Mark had finally promised to get his affairs in order. He was going on a long European tour, but when he returned he was going to write a will. Then he and Sabine planned to solemnize their relationship. Their future looked promising.

The End of a Dream

———————— ❧ ————————

RIGHT after Sabine and Mark bought the house, *Morphine* embarked on their European Tour. The group was in high spirits. They had a full program and were to play in many more music festivals. Things were going very well. They knew they were celebrities and were treated as such; they were making money. It was not just the three men, but they now had a whole entourage of necessary people such as managers, and lighting and sound professionals. Wives and girl friends were not invited when they were on tour, as Mark felt the band needed to concentrate on their work and should not be distracted.

After playing a few concerts, the band arrived in Palestrina, Italy, a town to the southeast of Rome. They began to prepare for their performance but they also became familiar with the town, its environs and its antiquities. According to the boys in the band, Dana Colley and Billy Conway, Mark had complained of being tired and out of breath. It was about 110 degrees Fahrenheit, however, and everyone was hot and tired. In addition, Mark had said something about his arm hurting. Neither he nor anyone else seemed to make much of this.

Morphine was the main feature at the big music festival in an outdoor park, the *Giardini del Principe*, in the center of the town. The stage was set up at one end and decorated with large sunflowers. The sound system was in place; the food stands were ready. Attendees were jammed together joking and in good humor. As usual, before the show Mark addressed the audience in Italian which was always a hit. And then the music began. When the second song started, Mark began to sing. Suddenly he fell backward, his bass still around him. Dana picked him up and held him. They lay on the floor surrounded by the sunflowers, which had been knocked out of their vases. Fortunately a cardiologist from the audience ran up to the stage until an ambulance came, but he told the boys he thought Mark was gone. According to

Billy and Dana, there was absolute silence. Everyone just sat for awhile, the lighting was turned down, the concert was cancelled, and the audience silently filed out.

Mark was pronounced dead at the hospital. The boys were distraught, grief-stricken, overwhelmed. People in the town reached out to them. The whole small town seemed dazed, sad and somber.

That night, July 3, 1999, we got a call on our answering machine from Deb Klein, Mark's manager. "Please call me whenever you get home. Call me at any time. I have news about Mark." I knew this could not be good news. When we called, Deb said:

"Mark's had a massive heart attack and he's gone."

"Gone? You mean dead?"

"Yes."

It did not seem possible. Bob and I both looked at each other in disbelief. We were shaking. It took a few minutes for the impact of this catastrophe to sink in; it was too much to accept. But then we had to get mobilized for what had to be done. Unfortunately, we knew all too well what was involved since this was our third son who had died, the third awful death with which we had to deal.

The phone calls soon began. After the festival manager notified Deb, she called us. Then we tried to call the boys in Palestrina to learn more details. By the time we made contact with them, it was four in the morning in Italy. They were waiting for our call in the lobby of their hotel near the park. On the phone, the boys cried and sounded confused when they tried to describe what happened and to make sense of it. Bob attempted to console them as he also tried to figure out what the next step would be.

We all had a lot to learn. According to Italian law, there had to be an autopsy because of the circumstances of Mark's sudden public death. It was arduous to arrange for the body to be brought back to the United States. Should we go to Italy? What could we do there? Deb and the festival organizers were handling the details and were keeping us informed. Although we were conflicted, Bob and I decided not to go at that time.

After Deb made sure that we got the news of Mark's death before we saw or heard about it on the media, she felt she had to reach Sabine for the same reasons. Sabine was on an island off the coast of Maine and had ridden her motorcycle there but left no number so they could not reach her. They had to send a message on the ferry for Sabine to call Deb's cell phone. Deb and Laurie, the drummer Billy Conway's girl friend, drove a pick-up truck through the night to tell her in person. It was a loving, difficult and tearful trip as she brought Sabine and her friends to Boston. Sabine's island friends brought the motorcycle back.

When Deb picked up Sabine in Vinalhaven and they were returning to Boston, Sabine tearfully and thoughtfully called us. Heart-sick, she wanted to share her grief with us. I was emotionally touched by her call.

Since we were stunned by this news of Mark's sudden death and were feeling displaced in our new home, it did not occur to me to invite her to stay with us. She said she had contacted her parents and that her mother was going to come down that day from Waterville Valley to be with her. Understandably, because she could not face going back to the loft herself, she and her mother booked a room at the Charles Hotel in Cambridge.

Mark's body was brought to Rome for the autopsy after which he lay in the hospital until he could be brought home. We called the American Embassy in Rome but the answering service there said the embassy was closed because it was a holiday. By then, it was the Fourth of July. "But this is an American holiday, not Italian!" we exclaimed. "Yes, but this is an American Embassy. It is a holiday for us." Eventually we got an inexperienced officer on duty who said he had never handled anything like this. In desperation, we called a friend who had been an ambassador in the Foreign Service. He kindly gave us some guide lines on what questions to ask and appropriate protocol

Meanwhile we had to find a rabbi and none was available. The senior rabbi at our temple had just assumed another pulpit and the new rabbi had not yet come. The assistant rabbi and all the other staff from our temple were on vacation or off for the week-end. We called the funeral home, which gave us the names of some of the rabbis on call and fortunately one of them, Rabbi Terry Bard, was a person we knew and liked, but he, too, was on holiday for the week-end. Fortunately, the funeral home contacted him, and he agreed to call us on Monday. Deb asked the European tour manager to oversee the details there, and then, when Mark was cleared, to accompany his body on the plane to the United States. Legally the body had to stay at the airport in Italy twenty-four hours before it could be shipped. Deb managed all the details and expenses for transporting the body. We were grateful.

Meanwhile the funeral home in Boston was in touch with the funeral home in Rome and arranged for the embalming and complying with other regulations.

Mark's body, or human remains, as the funeral home described him, finally arrived in Boston the day before the funeral. Then someone from the funeral home called us to ask if we wanted the coffin opened.

"Why?" I asked.

"To identify the body. Of course, you'd have to arrange for a welder to open the casket and then you'll need to purchase a new casket."

"No, just leave it as it is." I said.

This was more than I could handle. Mark had clearly died in front of crowds of people and his body had been under constant surveillance ever since. Neither Bob nor I doubted that the casket contained his body.

Eventually, Rabbi Bard came to talk to us about the final funeral details. He also enabled us to talk about Mark, his life and our relationships. This conversation was very helpful.

Prior to the funeral, we had contacted our out of town friends and relatives. Many had already heard about Mark's death and were ready to come to be with us and they did. We were sustained by the comfort and love they gave!

A few questions regarding the funeral still remained. By then Mark was a very public figure and we assumed there would be a crowd. In fact, there was standing room only in the temple. Therefore we arranged to have police manage the flow of people. As we walked in before the service, we heard Mark's music being played in the sanctuary. Bob, Martha, Sabine and I met with the rabbi in a side room as he said a prayer and cut the *crea* (the mourning ribbon) which we wore. Then we all walked into the sanctuary.

After the service, a long line of cars went to the cemetery. We even had a State Police escort. The police leap-frogged around the funeral entourage; they blocked the ramps on route 128 in order to keep the funeral procession intact.

The service at the cemetery in Sharon was brief. We all gathered on the grass around the casket before it was lowered into the ground. Bob, Martha, Sabine and I stood next to the rabbi as we intoned the usual prayers. Sabine tossed a silver bracelet with her name inscribed on it onto the casket as well as some flowers. We each threw a shovel of dirt on the casket as it was lowered into the ground. Then our family was ushered out. I wish we had stayed as the boys in the band finished covering the casket with earth. Afterward, since they had gotten permission from the rabbi to play some of Mark's music at the grave site, they got out their instruments and played his music after we left. People who stayed said it was very moving. It was a special tribute to Mark. Sabine said she realized what was happening and asked the limo to stop so that she could stay. I wished we had done the same as being there would have been important to us, but it did not happen.

The number of people who came from all over the United States as well as England, Ireland, and Belgium amazed us. Much to our surprise, one young cousin, Eric, and his wife Madeleine, flew in from Hong Kong. Many came back to our new home afterward to have refreshments and share memories as we began to sit *shiva*. Since Mark had just begun a contract with Dream Works, the president and others from the record label in California were in attendance.

Some of Mark's friends and colleagues introduced themselves and talked about how he had helped and encouraged them in their careers. He persuaded them to hold onto their dreams and to keep working and now some of them were achieving their goals. One of these was Chris Ballew who subsequently wrote the song "*Gone Again Gone*" a tender ballad in tribute to Mark.

Several others came over to me and said "I was often angry at Mark or I didn't always like him, but I'm sorry he's gone." I wasn't sure how to handle these comments, but I knew what they meant. Even at the funeral no one said he was easy. He was his own person, often self-centered, and always driven by his passions; he was confident about his vision and had principles to which he rigorously adhered.

As the day went on, I tried to do the right things. I greeted people, endeavored to understand their relationship to Mark, thanked them for coming and in the best way I could, attempted to be a good hostess. At least that was a familiar role for me. Furthermore, I was so numb I hardly felt tearful. I felt we had already been sitting *shiva* for a week before the funeral, and now had a whole other week to get through.

After everyone left, Bob and I had to face the following weeks. We were both stunned and totally exhausted. I was dealing with my own bewilderment over recent events and the devastation to our family. I felt acute grief for Mark and what he had lost, and what we, too, had lost. I was baffled by all the notoriety, since we really did not know much about his life at that time. We had no idea about the impact or import of his music. It was out of our realm of thinking. Subsequently, however, we have heard from other musicians that he was a "musician's musician", i.e. someone who felt, heard and performed a special, unique art.

In a way it was exciting to see the notices from all over the world, an article in the New York Times calling him a celebrity, his picture on the cover of the Phoenix and then long laudatory articles inside the paper. Radio stations played his music; clips of him were on television. Articles in newspapers and magazines spoke of his innovation, his genius, but also of the many ways he had helped and encouraged struggling musicians. We really had no idea of his contributions to the music world, and felt sad and guilty that we had not known more about him. I played his CDs over and over and for the first time got into what he was trying to do and heard his words and thereby his thoughts.

But at the time of his death, there were all the legal and business affairs that landed on us. Neither Bob nor I wanted any part of it. Because Mark was not married, left no will, and had no written contract with Billy, Dana and Deb, we were the next of kin and suddenly we owned *Morphine* and everything else that was Mark's. We wanted Sabine and the band to have *Morphine*; we did not want to have any of it. However, since there was no will, there was no way we could legally give it to them. It was ours whether we wanted it or not. Did we handle all his affairs well? Probably not. I really could not deal with any of it.

Fortunately, Bob is a doer and he rose to the task. It was he who dealt with the lawyers, stockbrokers, and accountants. We both could understand that the boys felt *Morphine* should be theirs. We did too, but our lawyers said we could not just give it to them. The whole situation was extremely complicated and stressful. I felt bad for them and Deb and Sabine. I also appreciated how sensitively and carefully they respected our feelings while at the same time they had to rethink and reshape their own lives. It was a horrible time for all of us.

Bob deserves much credit for reading books and learning about all the intricacies of the music world and managing Mark's estate. Yes, he made mistakes. Mark's stocks slipped drastically as we were dealing with other issues. The market was plummeting, but we had put this aspect of Mark's estate aside, assuming naively that the stockbroker was watching and would contact us. Of course, he didn't. We were in the clutches of the estate and entertainment lawyers who were annoyed with us for trying to give as much as we could to the boys. It took a long time to settle everything.

The hard part has been that in the midst of our grief over the loss of our son, we still had to clean up his business affairs. We felt angry about this. Mark was an adult and should have attended to these necessary details, but he procrastinated. Of course he always thought there would be a tomorrow; he did not expect to die. Still, for us, it was difficult to delve into the personal issues of a son who had been emancipated for many years.

What has complicated our mourning is that for years we had a conflicted relationship with Mark. We always loved him and wanted the best for him, but we frequently did not see things his way. Nevertheless, we now miss him terribly – miss his phone calls, his presence, his affection. But we surely wish he was around to manage his own estate.

Another aspect for us is that Mark's death was so public that we felt the whole world was grieving, which in a strange way took the privacy of our own grief and issues away from us. It was comforting to realize he was well-liked and respected by many and that his friends and even strangers we heard from were grieving. I wrote personal responses to all who had sent a note or donation in his behalf – hundreds of them – but it felt strange to send acknowledgements to so many people I did not know. Peoples' notes were impassioned and sincere or they would not have written, but the task of answering all of these, although therapeutic, was painful. I had to face over and over the enormity of our loss. However, compounding all of this was the fact that he was our third and last son whose death was untimely. Not only his fans and friends had in some way lost their hero but we had lost our son and it was our family which was now so diminished. Mark was gone now, dead, like his brothers.

It's now been twenty-eight years since Roger died and our family began to shrink. No one ever expected what befell us, but we are fortunate to have Martha and her family. Her story needs to be told.

Mark and Sabine 1999

SCALINATA

MARK ♪ SANDMAN

◂ MUSICISTA ▸

1952 ○ 1999

N.N.D.R. 2000

Plaque in Park in Palestrina, Italy

Our Only Daughter, Martha

ARTHA was our bonus baby — our cherished, loving, musical daughter. She was the flower in the family who grew from a shy little bud to bloom during her college years and finally blossom beautifully as she hit her stride and learned her strengths. In many ways she was and is my confidante and the daughter every mother wishes she had. The steady one in the family, she quietly stood in the background as our household reeled with Mark's acting out and with Roger's many problems. But she observed and was sensitive to what was going on and that influenced the way she reared her own children. Always a nurturer — she nurtured her dolls, her little brothers, her husband, her children, her students and now us.

Early on she had an ear for music. When we rode in the car, I used to sing in my atonal voice and noticed my little girl instinctively harmonizing. I could hardly believe it. It should have been no surprise that she chose to be a musician. Now a teacher of instrumental and vocal music in elementary school, she has an enormous repertoire of music and songs for all ages. Patiently she tunes instruments and leads chorus, band and orchestra. How did this reserved, self-effacing little girl become so capable and confident and a leader in her field?

She was the second born, the only girl in the bunch and our only surviving child, who has coped with losing her three brothers. I once said to her when I was feeling low that my life had not turned out the way I had anticipated. Her reply was, "Neither has mine!" Like all of us, she has been hurt but perhaps has achieved more than even she thought was possible.

I first learned about her when I went for my six-month check-up after Mark was born. Much to my surprise my obstetrician said, "Guess what? You're pregnant!" Yes, we wanted to have children close together but did not expect them quite this close. "Oh well," we thought, "babies for us are great whenever they come." We were really happy; our parents were stunned.

My pregnancy was easy with no complications. The real highlight for me was her birth. Because I felt I was hardly present at Mark's birth, I was determined to be awake for hers. In 1953, most women were anesthetized for their delivery. I suppose the doctors felt it was easier that way for everyone. I knew that was not what I wanted, so I told my doctor that if he would not do a natural delivery I'd look elsewhere. He was leery but agreed saying, "It's up to you. But remember, when it comes to the delivery I'm focusing on the baby and can't have you screaming and carrying on."

"I know what I'm doing and won't be a problem," I assured him and hoped I was right.

During my pregnancy I read and re-read Grantley Dick-Reade's book, *Childbirth Without Fear,* which was about natural childbirth. I knew with a one-year-old I was active and healthy, so I looked forward to the new experience. Once at the hospital, as my labor progressed, I was fortunate to have a nurse who had been trained at Yale where they were doing natural births. She was great and coached me with breathing and relaxing. She and the other nurses were amused because they were not used to having their patients awake and talkative. All of this seems anachronistic because just about everyone now has a natural birth.

It did not take long before the baby's head was starting to crown and they wheeled me to the delivery room. There the doctor said they had an anesthesiologist in case I needed one. They also strapped my hands down, which I felt was an indignity. I was annoyed but could not concentrate on that issue at the time. There were many people in the room – residents, medical students and nurses as well as the doctor – all curious to see how I'd do. The birth itself was exhilarating. They had arranged mirrors so I could watch. As soon as she was born, she cried and I heard, "It's a girl!" And there she was, all pink and gooey and covered with mucus, her face screwed up, her little fists flailing. As soon as the placenta was out, she was placed on my abdomen. I was euphoric. Here was this gorgeous new baby, the daughter I longed for, and all had gone so well. It was December 19, 1953.

Once she was washed and swaddled, our baby was brought to me. I thought she was the most beautiful baby ever. She was responsive and calm, eager to nurse. Bob and all the grandparents were thrilled to have this new little girl but I think I was the most grateful and gazed at her with disbelief that I could be so lucky. I was incredibly happy. We named her Martha Lee. Although this time Bob remained in the hospital, once I was in the labor room he was not allowed to see me until I was out of recovery. This too seems anachronistic.

It took about three months before Martha slept through the night but otherwise she was a contented baby and took her place in the family easily. I thought she was a beauty, my special daughter. In fact, once she was no longer a raw newborn, she did turn out to be a baby everyone stopped to admire. She had dark red curly hair, a ready smile and a sweet, friendly disposition.

It was hard to manage two children so close in age – almost like having twins except they were on different schedules. The challenge was to try to nurse her when Mark was awake since he never stayed in a playpen and was into everything imaginable. Often I'd put him in his room with lots of toys, close the door or gate to his room, and talk or sing to him as she was feeding. If he fussed I would send him messages, i.e. pictures or envelopes under the door, which seemed to keep him quiet.

Martha was not particularly active but she did walk on her first birthday and had a lot to say. Although she spoke early and not always intelligibly, she communicated with words before Mark did. Like Mark she also was stubbornly independent. For example, she refused to take a bottle and if I was out would simply fuss and go hungry rather than be fed, which was difficult for me. I nursed her for about six months after which she drank from a cup. Martha would not let anyone feed her. She'd grab the spoon and somehow, most of the time, get the food into her mouth and be happy and pleased with herself. Sometimes she'd take jars of baby food and try to drink the contents. What a mess!

Unlike the boys Martha was not a wanderer. She'd sit on the front steps or next to a window and watch the world go by. Also, she was resourceful, seemed to have a long attention span and loved books and puzzles and her dolls. She kept close to me and wanted to do whatever I was doing – she'd stir a batter of cookies or get diapers for her baby brothers or set the table or even polish silver. She was good company for me.

When Martha was two and Mark three we began to do family camping. At Nickerson State Park in Brewster, Massachusetts we rented a campsite with the tent already pitched and on a platform. There was a cache in the ground for an icebox and a fireplace for cooking. Since Bob and I had loved camping as kids, we were eager for the children to appreciate it as much as we did. At any rate, we got some air mattresses which we put on the floor, and settled into our tent. The little people got a thrill out of staying up late at night to see the stars and feel the quiet and beauty of an open campfire. We all had fun cooking and eating three meals a day out-doors. Even using the latrines was an adventure. I don't remember that we spent much time in the cold showers but we did usually have a swim in Crystal Lake where we got rid of the sand and salt from the ocean. That trip was the beginning of our yearly camping adventures. Of course over the years with more children and more camping gear, including our own tents, the camping became more complicated. Martha was our child who liked camping and roughing it the best and continued this tradition with her own children.

She was only two-and-a-half when Jonny was born. When Bob came to the hospital to take us home, Goldie was caring for Mark and Martha. Martha was standing on the sofa looking out the window when we came in the front door and ran over to greet us and to see her new brother. She was enthralled. She doted on Jonny, talked with him, tried to help.

After Jonny entered our family, Mark and Martha shared a room and got along fairly well. That time I had a baby nurse. As she was putting the rambunctious children to bed, she threatened, "You better be quiet or else!" I asked her what the "or else" would be. She said, "I don't know," but it had the desired effect.

A few years later, when Martha was in kindergarten, I got an irate call from a neighbor saying that Martha and her friend Nancy, had picked all her tulips. Our neighbor asked, "How could they do such a thing? Those flowers were my babies and they took every one. Now all my babies are gone." I said, "I'm so sorry. You should be angry. That was a dreadful thing for them to do. What can we do to try to make amends? I'll talk to the girls. I'm sure they did not understand what a naughty thing they did."

It was not like either little girl to get into mischief. When they came home from school I asked, "Why did you go into someone's yard and help yourself to all the flowers?" The girls started to cry and blurted,

"We thought they were so pretty and we'd take them to our teacher. We didn't know it was a bad thing to do." As I recall the teacher also called. She wondered where they had gotten so many beautiful flowers.

The tearful girls had to return to the scene of the crime, apologize and offer to help make amends. Our neighbor had calmed down by then but let them know they could not go in her yard again unless they were invited. It was a sad, sobering experience for the girls, which they never forgot.

Probably because she was so easy, Martha caused little commotion in the family. She was a particularly good sister to Roger and seemed to understand intuitively when he was having a hard time. When we went to Expo '67 in Montreal, we rented a tent trailer (our first adventure with one of these). We set off on our journey in the pouring rain (our family has a long history of vacationing in inclement weather). In the New Hampshire Mountains, with the car loaded with four kids and all our camping gear, we had a flat tire. Bob was quite calm, considering the circumstances, and replaced the tire. He did not use any expletives out loud. He refused our offers to help; he just told us to be quiet and not bother him. I remember passing out M and M's to try to keep the kids from poking at each other and quarreling. I thought if I gave each child his or her own package there would not be arguments. I was wrong. From the back seat I heard all of them complaining, "He has more red ones than I do" or "I didn't get any green ones."

When we got to the campground, it turned out to be the worst we'd ever seen. It was very crowded; there was no privacy as we were cheek to jowl with everyone else. Furthermore, the bathroom facilities were abysmal and muddy. The toilet stalls were so tiny you could barely turn around in them and the place was filthy. The fact that it was still raining did not improve our dispositions. We had a quick supper, which we tried to cook on our camp stove and ate inside the trailer.

Unlike the others, Martha tried to make the best of the situation. We settled in for the night in our very cramped quarters with six of us practically on top of each other. Because we were all so tired, we actually slept. Fortunately, the next day brought better weather and we were off to the World's Fair. It did not take long to realize that each of us was going at a different pace with different interests. Mark and Jonny paired. Protectively, Martha took Roger's hand and did what he wanted. She put her own interests aside to accommodate him.

Although Martha always liked music and dancing, she did not like to be programmed. She preferred to be more innovative. However, when Mark and Martha were invited to social dance classes in Newton we urged them to attend. The classes were called a cotillion and were rather formal. Often there was a supper at one of the homes before class. Mark seemed to sail through these classes with no problems. They were harder for Martha, possibly because she was shy but also, as I discovered, because she learned the girls were snobbish.

When it was my turn to drive the car pool I heard one of the girls say, in a condescending voice, "Martha, you're wearing the same dress today as you did the last time. Don't you have more than one dress?" Martha was quiet but I couldn't contain myself. "Cindy, that's not a kind thing to say. At your age, one party dress is all that anyone needs. If you have lots of party clothes that's very nice but not everyone does." There was little conversation in the car after that but I felt very sorry for my daughter. Understandably she loathed dance class.

I always thought Martha profited from healthy neglect. Because she seemed to be self-sufficient and well organized, she needed little prompting to do her homework, study her Hebrew or practice piano. She did what was expected of her, played with her friends and enjoyed her music studies. Early on it was clear that she was musical. She played recorder and then piano. She even enjoyed music theory. But what she really took pleasure in was singing.

My mother had been a fine pianist and singer. Some of my fondest memories are of standing around the piano on summer evenings as she played and my cousins sang or of falling asleep listening to her music. Mother had hoped I would have her abilities but I couldn't even carry a tune. Martha, however, could not only sing but took to the piano and actually had talent. She went on to play piano in the elementary school orchestra and then sang in the All-City Chorus. She continued to use her vocal talents to sing in the high school chorus. She had a good voice with accurate pitch but was not a loud or lusty singer so did not get into the dramatic musical productions she so wanted to be in. This was a big disappointment both to her and to us. Still, she kept trying and found other ways to be part of things. She even learned to play the flute and glockenspiel in order to be part of the marching band.

Whatever she did, she did wholeheartedly. I was her Campfire Girl leader for a few years but her closest friends were Girl Scouts, and she wanted to be with them. Once she joined, she seemed happier and more self-assured. She liked camping and "roughing it". She was not particularly happy at overnight camp until she went to Blazing Trail, a rugged YWCA camp in Denmark, Maine. There she made close friends and participated fully in all activities. Her comment was, "I met lots of girls from different backgrounds and different races. I learned that I liked some black girls but not others. Just like my friends from Newton." A good lesson.

During her high school years her relationship with Mark deteriorated. I suspect she was embarrassed by his behavior and upset by the tumult he was creating in our household. She tended to keep to herself, her bedroom door was often closed, and she did not show a lot of emotion. One time, however, when Mark and I were having a heated argument and I was crying, Martha came out of her room. Mark asked what she wanted and she said loudly and tearfully, "I can't stand what you are doing to our mother!" I don't know what else they had to say to each other but I think both Mark and I were stunned by her heated response to what was going on. Her high school years were certainly colored by all the tensions in our family.

I always thought that having a daughter would mean we could do "girl things" together. Probably not to my credit, I enjoyed shopping, cruising the stores and buying new clothes. This is something Martha has never enjoyed. When she was in high school I remember talking to her about current styles.

"You know hemlines are going up this year," I'd say.

"Who says?" was her reply. She surely was not and is not a creature of fashion. She has never been interested in clothes nor cosmetics. Fortunately she doesn't need artificial help.

After high school, Martha decided to go to Ohio Wesleyan University where she thought she would major in modern languages. That college proved a poor choice for her but she made the best of it. Her language study there was too easy and she did not like the geology and geography she had to take to meet her requirements.

To augment her social life, she joined a sorority. She knew her father was very involved with his fraternity at MIT and also that I rejected the elitism I thought the Greek organizations fostered. In fact when she invited me to come for "Mother's Week-End" in her sophomore year, she was uneasy. She said: "Mom, you're not going to like this.

There's a sorority reception for the mothers and you're expected to go."
She was right. I felt uncomfortable, not only with what I thought soror-
ities represented, but also with the "prissiness" of the affair. However, I
thought she was entitled to make her own decisions and for her this
was a good one. She liked the women there and felt part of the group.

While she was at Ohio Wesleyan, she realized that she really wanted
to major in music and that she could not get what she wanted there.
Bob and I took her to visit the Hartt College of Music in Hartford,
Connecticut as well as other conservatories. We were surprised by how
competitive, intense and dedicated the students seemed to be. I knew I
would have been overwhelmed in such schools but Martha seemed to
take the interviews in stride. Eventually she decided on the Crouse
College of Music at Syracuse University. Neither Bob nor I was impressed by Syracuse when we took her there but she seemed to be very
pleased and settled in right away. Martha majored in piano, voice and
music education and flourished there.

Years later she was angry with us and told us that we had always
made her feel dumb. "What do you mean?" we asked.

"Well, you were always after the boys to do their homework and to
get better grades and you never told me to do better. That made me
feel you thought I couldn't!" We were upset by her remarks. After all,
what we expected from each of our children was that they do the best
they could. It seemed to us that she completed her assignments
promptly and did not want to put forth the extra effort to get A's.
However, when she got into her major in college, it was clear that she
could and did excel far beyond her or our expectations.

At Syracuse, her interests in music, dance and Israel seemed to come
together and she spent two summers in Israel. Of all of us in the family, Martha seemed to be the only one really interested in all aspects of
Judaism. We had expected our children to complete their religious education and go through its important rites of passage. Each had a Bar
or Bat Mitzvah and was confirmed, but the boys did not want any further study. However, Martha did. After her freshman year of college in
1972, she went to Israel on a dance tour. She loved it. The next summer she was a counselor at Camp Young Judea. However, the following summer in 1974, she wanted to go to Harvard to take a course that
included another trip to Israel. We felt we had paid for one excursion
and that was enough. She seemed dismayed. To meet her expenses, she

applied to our temple for a scholarship, which she received. Then to supplement this she worked as a waitress at Vallee's Restaurant in Newton. It was hard work. Furthermore, her uniform challenged her. Either her stockings were slipping or her slip was showing or her red apron was awry. She hated and complained about the whole experience: the white oxfords she had to wear, the uniform, the inefficiency of the restaurant and the long hours.

The best part of the job, however, was the money she earned, especially the tips. Each evening she would come home, empty her pockets onto the kitchen table and count her money in front of us. She also learned a lot about people. Who were the big tippers? Who seemed appreciative of her service but left a minimal or no tip? Who were condescending to "wait people"? How much a smile or joke was appreciated! When she completed her stint at the restaurant and was getting ready to go to Israel, we offered to give her some spending money. She refused and said, "I can manage myself." And she did.

Her senior piano recital at Syracuse occurred in the middle of a very snowy winter. Nevertheless the whole family went, except Mark who was in Colorado. My father drove from Princeton to meet us in Boston. We took him, Goldie and Roger in our station wagon, which was loaded with food for the reception. To make the festivities, we brought gallon jugs of Cribari wine in red, white and pink, tablecloths, napkins, tins of homemade cookies and cakes and other goodies. Jon took a bus from Middlebury College and we picked him up in Albany. On our way to Martha's performance the car died. It just would not go. Fortunately we were not too far away from the recital hall, so we managed to pull to the curb and then lugged all the food and paraphernalia to the reception room. The recital was great and we were all very proud. Martha's friends happily drank and ate everything. The "*vin très ordinaire*" did not bother them at all.

The next question, of course, was how do we get home? The car had to be attended to and could not be driven. Therefore we rented a car for our return trip. Unfortunately, the rental car had no snow tires and the roads were covered with snow and ice. It was a memorable, scary, slippery trip back. Martha drove our car home a few weeks later without incident.

After college Martha spread her wings. She decided to get her Master's at McGill University in Montreal. She liked McGill and was planning to write her thesis on Ladino music, the music of the Spanish Jews from the 1400's, as she wanted a degree in ethnomusicology. Mid-way through the year, however, she was told that they had no one to supervise her thesis. This was aggravating and a huge disappointment to her but the year was not wasted. She had learned to make her way alone in a new culture; she excelled in her academics; she sang in a fine chorus, the *Studio de Musique Ancienne de Montréal*; and she grew up. Wherever she went she managed to be self-sufficient and always worked, usually by teaching in a Hebrew or Sunday school. These temples also offered her a community to be part of as well as some income. After Montreal, Martha went back to her then boy friend in Syracuse.

When she lived in Syracuse, she worked as a clerk in a music store. She told me she was amazed at the way people came in and asked for music.

"Do you have the piece that has a bright blue cover?"

Or "If I sing a little bit of a song can you find the music? I don't remember the name."

Or "I'd like the concerto in D minor that goes a little like this (hum) but I don't know the composer."

What felt remarkable even to her was that she usually could find the music. And that was in the days before computers and the Internet!

When she felt that Syracuse was a dead-end for her and her relationship cooled, she returned to Boston. She lived with a variety of friends and earned her living by giving piano lessons. By that time she was studying at the Kodaly Musical Training Institute in Watertown. She also was folk dancing at MIT where she met Ted Holmes, her future husband. Eventually they both joined Mandala, an international folk dance performing group. During this time, first Roger and then Jonny died. These were the brothers she was closest too. When they were little, she and Jonny paired off a lot; they both seemed grounded and organized. Martha had great empathy for Roger. She knew what he needed and gently helped him.

I've often wondered what was going through Martha's mind at the time, and what her feelings were. We never really talked about it. Martha was with us helping deal with all the details of sitting *shiva*. She handled the kitchen, took care of relatives and was gracious and sad. Everyone was sad. But Martha did not talk, or at least not to us. Bob and I were self-focused at the time. None of us spoke about our feelings. We were too numb to feel. Even today we wonder how Martha coped at that time. She had always gently assisted Roger. Was she angry now as well as sad? Was this a fair deal for the brother who had struggled so hard to succeed? What was her involvement with her brother's illness doing to her relationship with Ted? And where was that going? She did say at one point that Ted seemed to have trouble understanding how preoccupied she was with Roger's situation. "I told him my family needed me now, and that's where I'm going to be." – a forceful statement from her. I wondered if this untimely death was frightening to her. How had it affected her? Did it bring up the question of her mortality and the fragility of life? I wondered if she found solace in religion. Who was helping her deal with her feelings of loss and sadness? This was a tough one to deal with alone. I wish we had had the resources to be helpful to each of our kids at that time but we were too depleted to be of assistance to anyone. Although we tried, I suppose all of us were taking care of ourselves as best we could.

It was a hard time. Martha was trying to get her life in order after having put it aside while Roger was ill. She clearly was involved with Ted but we did not know what her plans would entail. Then Jonny had his accident and we were away. Somehow the emergency room at the hospital found Martha. She and Ted went to the hospital and then called Mark. It was clearly Martha, however, who took charge. Understandably, she was confused and upset but knew they had to reach us in Florida. Ted helped and actually made the call for us to come home immediately. They knew the situation was grave but had little understanding of all that was involved. When the call came from Ted, I had to confess that my biggest fear was that something terrible had happened to Martha. Somehow I felt that Jon had led a charmed life and that he would be O.K. I was wrong, of course, but those were my feelings at the time.

We couldn't comprehend what had happened but neither could she. We were full of questions and all of them were painful to contemplate. Each of us is haunted by them still. After her call to us, I was heartbroken and in a state of disbelief as we boarded the airplane to come home.

When we got to Boston City Hospital where Jon had been taken and put on life-support, we found Martha keeping vigil. She greeted us by saying, "I guess I'm next!" In fact she was the next oldest, but it was a horrible thought to me and obviously to her. I think Ted must have been overwhelmed by all the tragedies that were happening so quickly in our family and must have wondered if our bad luck was contagious. What was he getting into? How uncomfortable he must have felt with all the unfamiliar religious funeral rituals he was now exposed to!

Within five days Jonny was declared brain dead and we had to once again plan a funeral. Again the relatives and friends gathered. It was another untimely tragedy and I think those of us who were left felt jinxed and frightened.

Somehow we all got back into our usual routines. Bob seemed to cope but he found that he was inefficient and had trouble concentrating. Certainly, he was very sad and uncommunicative. I suppose I was too. Meanwhile Martha did not talk to us. Perhaps she was afraid to bring up her own grief because she thought it might exacerbate ours. Perhaps she just didn't have the words to do it. Perhaps she simply coped by denial – if you don't talk about it, it might go away – I don't know. Perhaps each of us had that wish.

It was only a few weeks later that Mark had his emergency surgery from his knifing incident a few years previously. Martha must have felt she had put her life on permanent hold when she finally said to us, "Mom, Ted and I want to go to San Francisco. I haven't been able to tell you because so much else has been happening. I know the timing is bad but we have to make our plans as well. I've been accepted at Holy Names College where I can complete my training in Kodaly and get my Master's and Ted thinks he can earn a good living."

We had been so consumed with all the crises and sadness around us that we had not been thinking about Martha. But we were taken aback with her pronouncement. Then we embarked on what was to be a poignant but wonderful turning point for all of us – her marriage to Ted.

Martha

Martha 1972

Martha and Ted's Wedding

───────── ❦ ─────────

I was surprised when Martha said she would go to San Francisco with Ted, although I should not have been. She and Ted had been seeing each other for several years; they had traveled together to Romania, Hungary and Yugoslavia; they were sharing an apartment in Cambridge. Making a more permanent relationship was the obvious next step but the timing was bad for them and for Bob and me. Our whole world recently had been full of catastrophes.

How could she go with no security, no formal commitment? Should she leave Boston and us at this time? Where would she get her support? Whom could she turn to? What would she do for money? Should she give up her full time job teaching in a public school just when her career was taking off? And what about us? Could we cope with the loss that her departure would bring? Should we encourage her, wish her well, hope for the best? What if she were not ready to make that commitment? What was in Ted's mind? What did he want? So many questions!

We got up our courage to discuss our concerns. She said, "We'd like to get married but there has been so much going on that there never seemed to be the right time to talk to you about it, so we just decided to continue to live together in San Francisco. We figured more permanent decisions could be made later."

I wanted Martha to be happy and cared for – I wanted her to be safely married to a partner she loved and who loved her. I was glad she had Ted. We liked him although we did not know him very well. He was quiet, shy and hard to engage in conversation but he was a good, strong, handsome man who was capable and very intelligent. He seemed to love Martha and she clearly loved him. Still, with this news I felt a sense of loss – a change, an ending and a sense of impending abandonment. I put my arms around Martha and hugged her tightly. Then more questions followed.

"Do you love Ted enough to spend the rest of your life together? – Have you worked out your religious differences? Have you thought through your plans? How you will get to California? And where will you live? How it will be for you so far from home?"

"Oh Mom, you always worry about everything. I'll talk to Ted. Maybe we should get married before we go but we want to leave in August and it's already the end of May. You know we can still live and make a life together without a wedding, without a formal marriage. Things will work out – I'll be OK."

"I'd feel terrible if you left with no more security than you have. Think about it. If this is what you want, we can get a wedding together pretty quickly but the most important thing to consider is your relationship and your dedication to each other. After all, you come from different backgrounds and cultures. Are you committed to making a life together? Will Ted be good to you as your husband? That's what is most important."

Then, a few days later they announced they were going to get married. Martha said she wanted to be married at home. At home? This was not something I'd thought about. I decided I'd deal with that later. Meanwhile, I don't recall Ted ever speaking very much to us nor us to him about any of this. He quietly seemed to go along with whatever Martha wanted. And we felt it was easier to talk to Martha about their plans.

Martha knew Bob and I had had an extremely small wedding and that I had always hoped she would have lots of friends and family present at hers. After a very short time it seemed she wanted a wedding too, although she was leaving most of the particulars up to me. Maybe she thought it would be good for me to have something positive to focus on. Suddenly, there were many details we had to face – a date, a rabbi, a caterer, the guest list, a tent, flowers, and a dress for Martha, a maid of honor, a best man and on and on. It really was fun to try to attend to all these things, though a bit stressful.

Martha was never one to obsess about the "what ifs". She had made her decision. For her, there was no looking back. However, I continued to worry. Like us, she was depleted emotionally. Was this a good time to make such a move? Did Ted have any security? Any job? How were they going to live? It all seemed problematic to me, yet for her this was a *fait accompli*. I felt she was entitled to her own life. I had to let go.

And I wanted to give her a good send off – one that would assure her of our support and love.

The first job was to find a rabbi. This was not an easy task since Ted's parents were Quakers. In fact his maternal grandfather was a Unitarian minister. Martha was definitely Jewish. However, in general, rabbis won't perform mixed marriages. Since I knew our own rabbi would not, I didn't even ask. That also eliminated the possibility of having the wedding in our temple. We consulted our friend, Rabbi Terry Bard, who had helped us after Jon died. He said he would do the wedding if he could have eight sessions with them and be sure they would have a Jewish home. If he did not think they would, he promised he would find someone for us. Martha and Ted agreed to see him for premarital counseling and subsequently Terry Bard agreed to marry them. The date was set for August 10, 1980.

Again I asked Martha about having the wedding at a hotel or some place other than home. She replied, "I want to be married at home. I want you to know that happy things can happen here. I love my home. This is where I grew up and we have a perfect setting. I know exactly where the ceremony will take place – it will be under the big oak tree in the back corner of the yard – we can get a platform and then stand under the trees which will make a natural *chupa* – (canopy for the wedding couple). It'll be great. Don't worry. It doesn't have to be fancy. We can even have potluck. Some of our friends have done that and it cuts out a lot of expense."

"Potluck! You have to be kidding. Can you really imagine us asking people to bring pot-luck for your wedding? You know I couldn't live with that. And whether the wedding is fancy or not, it's still a lot of work with many arrangements to be made. You're our only daughter and very special to us – we want you to have a proper wedding. It should be beautiful, gracious and gala – a good start for the rest of your life and a time you can look back on and feel good about."

"OK, you do it but Ted and I don't want people we don't know or like. Ted is adamant about not having people he doesn't know – he'd even rather not have extended family – he doesn't know them."

I was dismayed. I had always been close to several generations of my numerous cousins and we usually make a big effort to attend these meaningful occasions no matter where they are around the country. Also, we had many friends we would have liked to include. Nevertheless, this was to be her wedding and we had to compromise the best we could. I said,

"Well, we have lots of relatives we absolutely must invite. Ted and his parents can invite whomever they want."

"He has a small family and I don't think they'll come. It will probably be just his parents and his brother Ron. His sister is in the desert in California and is unlikely to make the trip. He has some cousins in New Hampshire who might come. I don't think his other relatives will as they don't live around here."

I thought about this for a moment. After all, this was Ted's wedding too. Then I responded,

"Do you think Ted will be overwhelmed by all of us? You know our family will gather and I want them to be with us. It is also important to have a few of our friends who have watched you grow up and are very fond of you. Probably only four families. That's really not negotiable. Otherwise you and Ted can have as many friends as you want. I'll call Mary and Ed (Ted's parents) about their list."

She agreed with this plan but still wanted to oversee the list of guests and said,

"You know we really want a lot of our friends so I'll show you our list. Then I want to see yours as well. We'll work it out. It will be hard for Ted but I think he will understand and go along with this."

"I can appreciate that this will be awkward for him and his parents – so many people they don't know – so many rituals that will be foreign to them. I'm afraid our family can be overwhelming. We'll try to make everyone feel included and comfortable. I guess the next step is to order invitations. They have to be engraved and that takes time."

"Oh no, Mom. Ted and I will make our own invitations. Don't worry about that."

"Make your own? What kind of invitation will that be? Is that proper? Shouldn't they be engraved and formal?"

"Trust me, Mom. What we make will be fine and it's what we want."

We let it drop and in fact they had a friend do the calligraphy for the invitations and then had them printed. It was not what I had in mind but they were fine. I doubt that anyone else cared.

"Martha, you know we have many friends who have been there for us over the past months and who would really like to wish you well too. What if we have a party for our friends and some family that we won't invite to the wedding? Would you and Ted agree to come?"

They said they'd participate. And so it went. We had a gala outdoor party for our friends inviting them to a CELEBRATION of the upcoming wedding. People seemed to understand and were eager to join us in a happy event for a change. We had colored lights all over the patio, which were a bit garish but festive. We hired a caterer, a friend of Martha's, and told her this will be mainly a Jewish crowd – they're hearty eaters but not big drinkers. The caterer said she understood. Alas, she didn't! We ran out of the delicious food but there was plenty to drink! An accordionist, a friend of Martha's from Mandala, strolled around and played familiar, lively music, which added a lot of vitality to the evening. It really turned out to be a most festive party and a good start to the celebrations that lay ahead.

And the wedding plans continued.

"Do you have a color scheme in mind?" I asked Martha.

"A color scheme? Who cares?"

"I do. I'd like it to be cheerful and happy – to me yellow is the sunniest color – could we have everything yellow and white – the tent, the flowers, and the linens for the table?"

"Sure, why not? You always did like yellow."

The plans rolled along. We settled on the guest list, ordered a yellow tent and began our search for a caterer. Since Martha had some other commitments, Ted agreed to interview the recommended caterer with me. At the Black Forest in Cambridge, we sampled some delicacies and thought they were good. They suggested we come to one of their weddings at the Lyman Estate to see how they presented their food.

"How can we invade someone else's wedding?" I asked.

"No problem. Just show up. There will be so many people, no one will notice."

So the next Saturday Ted and I, dressed in party clothes, went to the wedding of some unknown people. Everything looked OK to us although I was very uncomfortable being there. The food was artfully presented and quite light and delicious. We decided this would be fine and later signed an agreement for these caterers to do our wedding. They would provide lots of seafood, vegetables and a few meat dishes as well. A friend of Martha's would make the wedding cake. We agreed that we'd have only beer and wine at the bar. I really didn't have the energy to negotiate about prices. Did we pay too much? Should I have done more comparison shopping which I would ordinarily have done? I don't know. I just wanted to get things done.

Then a neighbor suggested Bachrach for a photographer. Neither Bob nor I had any knowledge about this so we went to Newbury Street to see their work. I knew they were a long-standing company and had a good reputation. Therefore we thought we couldn't go too far wrong. We signed for a photographer. This turned out to be a big mistake. The photographer was an elderly man who had no imagination or initiative. His pictures were not as good as the snapshots our friends took – although they were very costly. Since I had never arranged for a professional photographer before, I had not given him specific instructions, which was my expensive mistake.

We ordered some new plantings and shrubs for the yard and, of course, ordered yellow and white chrysanthemums to scatter hither and thither around the yard and patio and on the tables. Our gardener Tom, who was always a man of few words, got quite excited about having a wedding in "his yard". He even smiled and seemed more enthusiastic about his work. For fun, I bought large white trash barrels with painted flowers on the sides. We developed a contingency plan for rain. If necessary, awnings would be put up so people could get into the house. We decided our guests could stand around for the ceremony with a few seats in front for the elderly relatives. There would be tables under the tent for the meal. Martha was taking care of the music (we said to do whatever she wanted, whatever the cost).

In the yard, adjacent to the kitchen, was a fairly large bluestone patio. There was a stone retaining wall on one side, which offered a place to sit in addition to the lawn chairs sprinkled about. Further along on the grass was where we put the platform for the ceremony. The tent was to go on the other side of the stone wall.

Then I found a Mexican wedding dress. It actually was quite inexpensive but looked like something Martha might enjoy. It was layered, white, crinkled cotton and tiered with lace. What's more, it fit her perfectly. She insisted she show it to Ted to get his approval and once that was done, she was set in that department. The list of "to do" was finally shortening.

One of the final tasks was to choose the wine and champagne for the wedding. Martha and Ted did not seem to care and Bob and I were not knowledgeable about wines. At that time neither of us was a connoisseur of anything. Thus we consulted with our next-door neighbors, the Griesses. Ro's mother, in her eighties, and a total non-drinker, was with them at the time but joined the four of us as we sampled many bottles. After a hilarious evening enjoyed by all, Bob and I reeled home having chosen the most expensive wine and champagne.

Two days before the wedding I looked down from our bathroom window and saw a large pink and white tent starting to be erected. I couldn't believe my eyes. I ran downstairs and asked, "What are you doing? This isn't what was ordered. I ordered a yellow tent – everything is going to be yellow – we can't have a pink tent – it will ruin everything!" The tent people said this was what they'd been given. I told them to stop and I'd call the company. I retrieved our contract, which very clearly described what was ordered and made the call.

"Well, the yellow tents we had were not in good condition so we substituted this one. It's a new tent. It will look very nice."

"I don't care if it's new or not but it's not what I ordered. It's your responsibility to provide the right item. We have to have a yellow tent today or tomorrow – you'll just have to buy one if you don't have it."

I could not believe I was talking like that. I was hysterical. At any rate, the tent people got my message and much to my relief, a spanking new yellow tent soon covered the lawn.

Finally people began to arrive from around the country. I was very excited but still apprehensive about all the details – were all the bases covered? Would the caterers arrive on time? Would the musicians and the photographer come?

Since so many out of town relatives were coming, we had to find something to do the night before the wedding. Ted's mother said it was too bad she couldn't do anything because they did not live locally. Actually they had just returned from their assignment in Ghana where they were in the diplomatic service. That left dinner up to us. Fortunately, Bob's sister and mother rose to the occasion and hosted a very extravagant and festive dinner at the Hyatt Regency Hotel in Cambridge. Bob's sister, Jo, is an expert on details and has wonderful taste. The tables were set with black multi-flowered tablecloths. Bright, colorful floral arrangements perched on each table. Everything was done to perfection from the hors d'oeuvres to dessert. One of my cousins suggested that we have each guest stand and say how they were related to the bride or groom. This turned out to be a great icebreaker. Some were serious but most had funny anecdotes or described convoluted relationships. Everyone loosened up and had fun.

Suddenly it was the wedding day. I looked out the window and saw it was clear and sunny. I opened our kitchen door and there was a cool breeze. I couldn't believe it. The 90 degree heat we'd had all week had left and there was no rain. It was a perfect day. Martha had spent the night at home and was very calm when she got up. Before long the caterers arrived and took over the kitchen. Then Mary, Ed and Ron arrived as did Mark in his new high styled suit and tie. We were all dressed and staying out of sight as we peeked out the living room doors to watch our guests come through the garden gate. I was very excited and moved to see our families and close friends gather. Martha and Ted were glad to see all of Mandala, their performing dance group, and many of their other friends as well. And then it was time.

At the last minute we gazed out the glass doors at the assembled crowd. Mary was adjusting Martha's hair and flowers and seemed very fond of her. I thought Martha looked beautiful. She carried the ornately covered Bible that had been in my mother's family for generations, the same one I had carried at my wedding. There was a small bouquet on top. She was the calmest of us all as the photographer took a few pictures of us, and included Mark and Ron as well. Rabbi Terry Bard arrived and led the procession into the yard and onto the platform and the ceremony began.

I was keenly aware of the eyes on us and most particularly on me. It was no secret that we had had a difficult few years – especially the past few months. Everyone seemed attuned to our feelings and I felt people were gazing at us to see how we'd hold up. Mary, Ed, Bob and I were on the platform with the matron of honor and best man. The rabbi performed the ceremony under the bower of trees as planned; the glass was broken and the music began. There was lots of music – Martha had a guitarist, a violinist and a brass quintet. I don't even remember in what order they played but it was great.

Did I cry? Did I think about the boys who would have wanted to be there? Did I wish they were there? Of course. Did I ache and wish my parents could have savored this moment? Yes. Did I break down and cry? NO. I was afraid if I let any of the tears that welled up inside come out, I could not stop the flow. So I remained self-contained and bottled up inside. People were watching me and I was determined to make this a happy day for Martha with no tears.

Everything seemed to work out well. The bar was at one end of the tent and buffet tables on one side of the tent and replenished as needed. There were lots of little sandwiches, dips and other appetizers for starters. Then there were salads of all kinds, plus meat and seafood kebabs. I don't remember what else. Certainly no one could go hungry. A friend of Martha's had made an enormous *chale* loaf of bread, several feet long. The rabbi made a blessing, a *motzi,* and as called for by tradition, the bread was broken and passed around.

And it was a joyful day. Mark, who was neither suave nor used to formal affairs, offered a toast to the bride and groom for their happiness together and future good fortune. I don't remember his exact words. I think they started with "Here! Here! Let's raise our glasses for Martha and Ted," but the right sentiment was there and everyone chimed in.

The Mandala group, some of whom came in folk costume, helped to make it special. They were not only dancers but also good musicians and not at all inhibited. Every now and then they would break into song. Finally they said, "Let's dance!" They led a snake like line away from the tent, around the house to the other side, where there was a large open lawn and we danced following their direction – not only the *hora,* the traditional Jewish wedding dance, but also all kinds of line dances from other countries. It was wonderful and exhilarating and joyous – just as I had hoped.

At the end, Martha and Ted wanted to serve ice cream. We had gotten some of their favorites and finished the day with that. Meanwhile our kitchen was awash with what the caterers had left. It was easily mopped up and by around six o'clock the last guests had left.

It might not have been the most traditional nor the most proper wedding but it was Martha's wedding and our little girl, the young woman who was so dear to us, was now married and about to start a new phase of her life – and to leave us. Nothing would be the same but we were happy for her. She clearly was excited about her move to California – It was to be an adventure – She seemed happy and devoted to Ted – What more could we ask for?

A few days later they set off for their trip in Ted's van, which was tightly packed and amazingly efficient. I was impressed with their careful planning and attention to detail. And they were very excited as they set off for their new life together! As we waved good-bye and the car went out of sight, we were happy for them but felt abandoned, empty and sad.

On the way to California they stopped at the homes of relatives, even some distant relatives, who graciously took them in. The hospitality these relatives extended to family, whom they didn't know very well, was a surprise to Ted.

I suppose all endings are beginnings of something else. As this story continues, Martha and Ted's new life brought special joy to us as well as to them.

Martha and Ted August 10, 1980

Our Family Begins to Grow Again

❧

IT's not unusual to experience a let down after all the excitement of a wedding. And so it was for us, especially after everything else that had gone on during the year. However, our lonely feelings were more than ordinary. Yes, Mark was around but appropriately independent. He was very much into his own affairs, living on his own, working, taking courses at U. Mass. Boston and being with Toni. Martha, who had always been in close contact with us, was now embarking on an exciting new period in her life but was far away.

It felt like we had lost our whole family. Because we needed to be busy and with people, we both immersed ourselves in work and tried to socialize with friends. Nevertheless, we aimlessly rattled around in our big house that was full of memories and now was so terribly quiet and empty.

While our family as we knew it had drastically changed, Martha's marriage and having Ted for a son-in-law began a new chapter for us all. I worried about how they would manage as they settled into the day-to-day issues of making a life together. How did it feel to them to be far from their usual supports of family and friends? As parents we were concerned about them but essentially had faith in their sound judgment. Since we were no longer part of their daily lives we wondered what, if anything, they were going to share with us. We wanted to know how they were settling in, who their new friends would be, what were they doing for fun. We hoped they'd keep in touch and share some aspects of their lives with us.

Martha and Ted settled into Oakland, CA. They lived first in an apartment and then bought a small fixer-upper house, also in Oakland, with the Berkeley Hills in the background. They seemed to make friends easily through Martha's school, her jobs teaching Hebrew and music and Ted's work, which he mainly chose to do at home. They also developed strong friendships with their neighbors and joined Westwind, a folk dance group that they both enjoyed.

Much of their time was devoted to updating their home. Ted had always liked making his surroundings more attractive, economical and functional. With great gusto and grit, they washed and painted walls, built a new kitchen and added on to their bedroom. They chopped up the cement that covered their back yard and replaced it with fruit trees and plants, vegetables and flowers. On the side of their house they placed a magnificent rosy colored bougainvillea, a gift from Martha's cousin Kamala Asher, which covered the entire façade. Ted did most of the wiring and plumbing himself as well as the kitchen cabinet work. In addition he made the foundation of the house earthquake proof, which was backbreaking work. All of this happened over a period of years.

It took a while for us to get to know Ted. He had entered our family at a stressful time of enormous upheaval and neither Bob nor I was able to give him the attention he deserved. That might have been OK with him, because he is a very private person. However, it was not OK with me. I wanted to get to know him better, to understand their relationship, to learn more about his ambitions. But now they were no longer geographically close and our visits would be more intense and therefore it would be harder to have relaxed conversations. What I did understand was that like Bob, Ted is an engineer, and less interested in developing relationships than in learning and doing. He had degrees in both mechanical and electrical engineering and he was extremely proficient in computer languages and computer hardware as well. Ted liked to make things work properly and could not stand inefficiency or poor workmanship, so he usually preferred to fix things himself, even though there were often several projects going simultaneously. He was and is a perfectionist. I continue to be awed by his many abilities and am convinced there is nothing, given the time and resources, he cannot fix or make.

Bob has many of the same characteristics, although Bob does not like to tinker with things very much. He's a perfectionist in whatever is important to him. Both Bob and Ted tend to keep their feelings to themselves; both want to be left alone when they don't feel well; both deny pain; both have strong political views albeit different from each other. Some things, we've learned, are better not discussed. But both do have a social conscience and are generous in volunteering their time and energy. Neither has tact as his strong point. Over the years, my observation is that Ted has become more expansive and Bob less so.

During the time they were establishing their home, we were hoping for grandchildren. Then in the fall of 1982, we got an excited call from Martha. "Mom, I have good news. I'm pregnant!" Indeed that was the best news we could hear and the best we had had in a long time. We were thrilled and hardly dared to believe our good fortune. Martha and Ted were planning to come to Boston for Thanksgiving. I could barely wait to see and hug her. When she came, however, she had a lot of pain and was feeling ill. She ended up in the hospital where she was evaluated and had to spend the night. The next day she called and said, "I hope you're sitting down. I'm fine but in a state of shock. The doctor just told me I'm not carrying one baby. I'm having twins!" Bob and I (and I think Ted) were elated; she was overwhelmed. Of course with this announcement also came some worry. What do grandparents-to-be think about but the health and well being of their children and grandchildren? All we could do was hope that they would be healthy and she would have an easy time.

In fact, she had a hard pregnancy because she had large fibroid tumors that grew at the same rate as her babies and caused her considerable pain. She had to stop working at four months. Then on the evening of May 27, 1983 the call came from Ted. They had two little boys named Alexander and Gabriel. Ted said that Martha had an emergency C-section but that the babies were fine as was she. Our hearts overflowed with joy and gratitude. This was the news we had been hoping and waiting for! Two brand new lives to give us something positive to focus on, when for so long we focused on life's sorrows. After we contacted family with the good news, we woke our neighbors the Griesses, who came over in their pajamas to rejoice with us as we dipped into some of the leftover champagne from the wedding. What a lovely new beginning and cause for celebration!

Since my offer to help after the babies were born was accepted, I flew to California the day Martha and the babies were to be discharged. From the airport where Ted picked me up, we went directly to the hospital. And there they were! Martha looked tired, a bit nervous but happy. The nurse was dressing and swaddling the two tiny babies. The little boys were full term but Gabriel, the older and smaller one who weighed less than five pounds, fit in the palm of my hand. As she was being discharged, Martha was told that the babies were fine. She just needed to keep a cap on Gabriel and to feed each of them every few hours as they cried. Then we were off. Unfortunately there was only one car seat. What to do? Our solution was to put them both in the one seat where they fit easily. All was quiet on the way home.

Once we arrived the boys were no longer quiet and Martha was sore and exhausted. We knew we had to establish some routines. In the boys' room were a bed, a full-sized crib, a dresser with a pad on it for a changing table and a rocking chair. The crib could accommodate both boys crossways and we laughed as they seemed to inch toward each other and often would end up practically holding hands. The big project, however, was trying to remember who was fed and when. Eventually we set up a chart so that we could document which baby was fed, at what time and on which breast. I stayed in the boys' room so that I could change them and have them ready for Martha to nurse. Since the babies rarely were awake at the same time, it seemed that we'd just get one settled when the other would wake up and we'd have to start all over again. None of us had much sleep.

For the next two weeks, I was "chief cook and bottle washer". I did loads of laundry, marketed, cooked and helped with bathing and changing the boys. I tried to accommodate Ted and Martha's life style. Although they had a dryer, they preferred to save electricity and hang clothes on the line out-doors. Therefore, every day the line was full of tiny shirts and nighties along with sheets and blankets. Martha and Ted liked their food prepared from recipes from the Moosewood Cookbook. I liked these recipes too but they required lots of chopping time and often special ingredients. Taking care of the babies in order for Martha to get some rest was the easy part. Fortunately they had a diaper service since the pile of diapers was staggering. I thought at that crucial time we should have taken advantage of modern conveniences and conserved our energies for more important things but I was alone in my ideas and did not want to make waves. I certainly did not want to be an intrusive mother-in-law.

After about a week when Martha was feeling better and the boys had been fed, I suggested she and Ted go out for a walk and some ice cream. I was sure I could manage since at that moment the boys were asleep. Martha and Ted had no sooner left than both babies awoke simultaneously and began to scream. It was bedlam. Now what should I do? First I checked each one and decided there was no real crisis. I put one baby in a little swing that moved gently back and forth. That soothed him. Then I picked up the other howling little guy, gave him some water and walked around with him. Eventually, I alternated the babies on the swing and on my shoulder. Oddly enough, when their parents returned all was calm and serene.

The time went by quickly and I wished I could have stayed longer to help but I had to go back to work. Bob wanted to meet the babies, so he came the last weekend before we went home together. Since I really wanted to stay and bond with the children as well as to help Martha, it was hard to return to Boston and a wrench to say good-bye. Although I have never been so tired, I was also very excited about what lay ahead. On the way home in the plane Bob and I got out the many pictures we had taken of these little miracles and their parents. We chuckled and glowed with pleasure as we looked at the pictures. It felt so good to smile and laugh again.

At that time, Ted worked from home and was a huge help and the extra hands Martha needed. In order for Martha and Ted to have a respite, they hired a high school girl to come for a few hours daily to take the babies for a walk. Even with this assistance that first year, according to Martha, was a blur. It was so busy there was no time to think. You just had to do.

I remember one visit when Ted sat the two tykes on the kitchen counter in little bouncy seats. It was an assembly line. He had one jar of baby food and shoveled the food into one mouth and then the other, all with the same spoon. The boys chortled and laughed and spit the food out, which he shoveled back in. It was quite a sight but no one was unhappy.

When they were four months old Bob and I went to their naming, a ceremony in which Jewish children are given their Hebrew names. We went to their temple on a Friday night. Martha and Ted held the two boys in different colored velour jumpers, one blue and the other yellow with white turtlenecks, as the rabbi blessed them. During the service the boys were laughing, kicking and egging each other on so the congregation could hardly keep a straight face. I have no idea what blessings were said. It really did not matter. It was such a joyful moment.

The choice of their Hebrew names, however, had been an issue. In the Jewish tradition, a child is named after someone special who has died so that his or her soul will live on. Apparently there is another part of the tradition that states that you should not name a child after someone who has died tragically, since that might bring bad luck. This was a dilemma for Martha. Despite this she decided to give the boys the Hebrew names of her brothers, their uncles. I doubt that Ted cared about their Hebrew names but Bob and I did and were glad she had made this decision.

Once when the boys had just started to walk, they all came to visit and met me at the hospital where I worked. The boys squealed in delight when they eyed the long corridors the hospital offered. As soon as they were put down they scooted off in opposite directions, elated with the space. It took several of us to corral them. I think afterwards they had harnesses, which might have cramped their exuberant style but which made them more controllable.

We felt very fortunate that we were able to visit on one side of the country or the other every few months. I longed for a more relaxed relationship but we did the best we could at the time. Each visit was short and intense whether it was on their turf or ours.

After seven years in California, Martha wanted to return to Boston. The boys were four and she said she preferred the schools and life on the east coast. I think she also wanted to be closer to family, although she did not say this. I could understand why Ted was unhappy to leave Oakland and Berkeley. He liked the casual life style, his men's group and their friends. He had also established his own clientele there although I think the nature of his work was portable. However, in the summer of 1987, they moved east. Because of all the improvements they had made on their home, they were able to sell it at a good price, which enabled them to purchase a new home here.

They stayed with us that summer until, much to our surprise, they bought a small house not far from us in Newton. This house, like theirs in California was a fixer-upper but in a good school district, near the MBTA stop and on a dead end street. The Newton house and its neighborhood have worked out well for them. They settled into it easily, updated and remodeled it. Whether they knew it or not, their being so close was a huge, unbelievably delicious gift to Bob and me.

As soon as they moved, Martha got a position as the music teacher at the Lawrence School in Brookline. Two years later she began work as the music teacher at Temple Israel in Boston where she worked for seven years. This enabled the boys to begin their religious education and also provided her with extra income, but it also meant that she worked six days a week. It took a little longer for Ted to find what he wanted and to get established. At first he free-lanced but for quite a few years he has worked mainly at Intex Solutions and now is on their full-time staff. His colleagues as well as the challenges and projects with which he's involved stimulate him. His talents are clearly appreciated and he seems happy.

After a few years, much to their surprise and pleasure, Martha learned that she was pregnant again. My impression was that Ted was stunned but Martha was glad. She became even happier when she learned that she was only having one baby and a girl. As a treat for me, Martha invited me to join her when she had her ultrasound. I had never seen this and felt excited and privileged to see this new little life swimming around *in utero*. Knowing the gender of her baby ahead of time enhanced Martha's joy, for this would be the little girl, the daughter I believe most mothers want. While I always thought it was fun to hear "it's a girl" or 'it's a boy" when the baby was born, I have to admit that knowing early really seemed to cement the bonding. I was grateful she let me share the experience.

Once again, Martha had a difficult pregnancy because of recurring fibroids. Still, she worked until a few days before Amanda was born on October 17, 1990. It was a chaotic time. When Amanda was two weeks old she became very fussy and feverish. The doctor was so concerned about her that she hospitalized the baby for hydration and observation. This meant that Martha had to stay in the hospital with her. Meanwhile the boys had stomach upsets and Ted was trying to manage the home front. Fortunately, Amanda's symptoms subsided and the boys felt better, but it was a tense few weeks.

Since Martha planned to return to work after her maternity leave of a few months, I offered to take care of Amanda one or two days a week. She turned down my offer and said she'd prefer to save us for emergencies. I don't think she realized how disappointed I was. I wanted so much to be needed and to take on this responsibility but I had to respect her decision. She did call on us quite a bit which was always a welcome treat, since Amanda was a sweet, responsive baby and toddler. The bonding with her was comfortable and easy.

About six months before Amanda was born, Ted wanted a dog. Therefore, before long, Leo, a honey-colored cocker spaniel puppy joined the family. He was a frisky little dog and very protective of Amanda especially once she began to crawl. If I was at their house and went to pick her up, Leo would dash over and sit on her legs and dare me to touch her. Unfortunately, fifteen years later Leo had to be put to sleep. He was blind, deaf and arthritic. He also had tumors. However, his sense of smell was fine and still drew him to the kitchen where he hoped for some treats. No one wanted to say good-bye to him. Martha, Ted and Amanda held him as he died and not only they, but also the veterinarian wept. It was like the death of another family member and certainly the end of an era.

Living so close by while the children were maturing, we were able to attend their concerts, games and school performances. Their many accomplishments continue to astound us. All of them are musical. Alex and Gabe both had starring roles in their Middle School's production of *Lil' Abner*. Alex played oboe and Gabe the cello; both played electric guitars and had their own rock band. In addition, the boys were soccer players and on the Varsity team in high school, where they were skillful aggressive players. I cringed when I watched them play, since it seemed too rough as they banged into other, hit the ball with their heads and often had bad falls.

Amanda began to play oboe in the fourth grade. I remember going to her first concert that spring when the school band performed. She, like the other children, was very proud and excited. The auditorium was packed on that hot, stuffy June night with many doting parents and grandparents. Then, as the conductor lifted her baton, the first notes sounded. It was like the "think system" from the *Music Man*. Everyone was out of tune and played at his or her own pace. The children however, were earnest, intent and pleased with themselves. Meanwhile, people in the audience tried to keep from laughing. Of course, the applause was loud and enthusiastic.

Now Amanda is involved with singing groups. She sight-reads music well and is not afraid to audition for local and national choruses; often she is accepted. Since she cannot be in both choral and instrumental music in school, she had to choose and preferred her choral groups. Like her mother, she has true pitch but a soft voice, which we hope she can develop. What matters most is that she enjoys singing.

Almost more important to us than the achievements of her children is what Martha has accomplished. She is no longer the shy, self-effacing little girl we had known or the rather gauche new teacher we had seen in her first job in Townsend, MA. Surely she had done a good job there but she was a new teacher. We relished her ability to conduct her choruses but felt she did not connect to her audience very well.

After she got her Master's degree in California and returned to Newton, however, she gained self-confidence and displayed her expertise. She worked with the children in Brookline, presented her concerts with increasing confidence and showed more control and connection not only with her students but also with their parents. It was clear she was invested in her work and the kids really liked her.

Then she got a position teaching music at the Williams School in Newton. There she came into her element. Her vast repertoire of songs as well as her expertise enabled her to develop her own program for all the children. Each year when we went to her Harvest Festival and saw her lead every grade from kindergarten through fifth grade with age appropriate songs we could hardly believe this was our shy little girl. She is a tough, truly gifted teacher, who demands order, but tempers that with her palpable respect and love for the children. We are very proud of her. What greater calling could she have?

She has many other special qualities. I have mentioned that she is a doer. She is very unlike me. When she sees something that needs to be done she attacks it. The walls need to be re-painted so she does it during spring vacation. She wants to make a quilt for a friend's new baby. Quickly and without fanfare a quilt is done. Someone is sick and needs a meal – she provides a casserole or a full meal. If Bob or I become ill, she comes with hot soup or a casserole and flowers. She responds to what is needed and does. It is admirable and awesome to me.

I don't understand where she gets her energy. She seems to be clear about her priorities. She takes care of her household, her children, her career and still manages to find time and energy to be concerned about us as well as Ted's parents. In my opinion, she is amazing and would not like us to say this about her.

Being part of the lives of Martha, Ted, Alex, Gabe and Amanda lightens our sorrows and is what keeps us going. It certainly is what makes our lives worth living. What is more important than the next generation? We're glad they include us. They are our legacy and our love.

Martha, Alex and Gabe

"Uncle Mark" with Alex and Gabe 1984

Amanda and Martha 1995

"Uncle Mark" and Amanda 1998

The Holme's Adventure in Costa Rica 2007
Martha, Amanda, Ted, Alex and Gabe

WHAT ABOUT FAITH?

––––––––– ❧ –––––––––

MANY people who have endured hardships turn to their faith. We have not been able to. While we are certainly cultural Jews and value our ethics, traditions and rituals, we, or at least I, do not have much faith in God. I don't understand God and wish I did. When for many years I was a social worker in oncology, I observed patients who had a deep faith in God and in the hereafter. It seemed to me that they dealt more comfortably and peacefully with their issues of serious, life-threatening illnesses than those who did not have an unquestioning belief. Frequently a patient would ask me to pray with her. Since I do not pray I found this difficult. Nevertheless, I would hold her hand and sit quietly by her bedside as she prayed. We did not need spoken words. Prayer, as her way of communing with God, was personal but to have someone share the moment and experience seemed to comfort and reassure her. I wished that, like her, I had such a strong faith. It seemed to give her solace.

I suppose most of our religious beliefs go back to our childhoods. In my home, my mother talked about Judaism as the basis of what we do and how we act, but faith, or spirituality was not talked about. When I was small, my mother would come to tuck me in at night and we would say a prayer. I didn't know what it meant but it was part of our good-night ritual and having my mother share the time with me was comforting. However, the prayer worried me. The prayer was: "Now I lay me down to sleep, I pray the Lord my soul to keep; if I should die before I wake, I pray the Lord my soul to take". This common child's prayer, although I don't think it's a Jewish one, frightened me. Was I going to die that night? What was my soul? Who was this Lord? Why did I have to say this? Did it mean my future was out of my control? Looking back, I realize I was compliant. There were many unasked questions and, unlike in many Jewish homes, I was not encouraged to ask.

Every night I also said the *shema* in both English and Hebrew. *Shema Yisrael Adonai Eloheinu Adonai Echod* – Hear, Oh Israel, the Lord is our God, the Lord is One. This was a mantra for me. We then finished our prayer with part of the *Veahavta* – You shall love the Lord your God with all your mind, with all your strength and with all your being. I did not know that these words were part of the guiding principles of our faith. I learned only recently that the *mezuzahs* on the doorposts of every house where I've lived contained these words on a tiny scroll of paper. Growing up, I didn't think much about what I was saying. They were just words which I recited, but they did make me feel secure.

Later, however, when I did read them in our prayer books, I knew that they resonated from somewhere in my past. Since my mother never gave the prayer a name, all I remembered were the words said before going to bed and they felt familiar and comfortable. Today these words are still a mantra for me.

My mother made a Jewish home. She kept kosher so that her in-laws would visit and also because that was the way the way she was brought up. Every Friday she blessed the Sabbath candles and we had a traditional Sabbath meal of chicken soup with fine noodles, roast chicken and soft, sweet challah bread. On Saturday we had a cold lunch of leftovers. While my father knew all the prayers by heart, he did not say *kiddish* on Friday night. He visited the cemeteries every year, said *kaddish* for his lost relatives, and went to services on the high holidays. Although he could easily recite the prayers, he was not a religious or pious man. I doubt that my father questioned much. He just tried to do the right things and to be a good man.

Remembering the dead was an important obligation for both of my parents. Every September, they took me along with them to make the rounds of various cemeteries in Pennsylvania where his parents and my mother's, as well as many of her siblings were buried. They would find a Rabbi to say a prayer and then leave a stone on the gravestone. Also, there always seemed to be a *yahrzeit* candle burning in memory of some relative. This is a tradition I continue. I find the flame that lasts twenty-four hours reminds me of the life that is now ended.

It seemed to me that my parents were bound by tradition but did not emphasize or even talk about spirituality. Rituals and prayers were meaningful to them but they did not explain them to me.

When I ask Bob about his faith he rarely has much to say. I ask, "Do you really believe in God? How do you pray? How does it make you feel? Do you think prayer helps?" His replies are evasive but he says, "Yes, I believe in God and I do pray. However, I don't obsess or question what I believe like you do." My impression is that he goes through the motions and finds some solace in that. He had a religious education and knows biblical history but until recently never was interested in studying Talmud or Torah. His family celebrated the Sabbath with festive dinners and I think Bob's father, David, made a point of being home early on Friday nights but my impression was that they were not particularly spiritual.

In order for the children to know more about their background and heritage, we thought it was important for them to go to religious school and prepare for the Jewish rites of passage. Regrettably, we dropped the children off at temple and did not re-enforce much at home. Their experience would have been so much more meaningful if I had studied along with them, but I didn't.

What we tried to do within the family was to talk with the children about the importance of Jewish ethics and values – values such as having a social conscience and being caring, honest, trustworthy people. As best we could, we tried to be good models for them. We celebrated all the holidays and festivals and I know the children always particularly enjoyed Chanukah and our Passover Seders. Unfortunately, we did not have a Sabbath dinner, partly because by Friday Bob was tired and found it hard to get home early. This was an issue between us. Since we were trying to make a Jewish home, I thought we should try to make the Sabbath special but it was not important enough for him to make the effort to do this. Eventually, I lost interest too. Therefore we rarely went to Temple as a family, except of course on the high holidays.

I wish now that we had been more observant and made Judaism more appealing to our children. I believe that if Bob and I had been more mature and had worked out more clearly how we wanted to rear our children we would have given them a more solid foundation. I do not think I would have had a kosher home but lighting the Friday night candles, saying or singing *Kiddish* and making Friday evening special would, in my opinion now, have given our children a better connection with their heritage. When I was a child the Sabbath was a day of prohibitions, such as don't write, or don't ride your bike, or don't use scissors or sew or knit and I often cheated on these rules. Since I had never experienced the joyfulness of Judaism or the Sabbath at home and was also conflicted about what I wanted and since Bob didn't seem to care, we did not observe these traditions.

Thus, although we were Jews, I never had much faith in God. Although my extended family was quite orthodox, I had no formal religious training. To give my parents credit, they tried to give me a religious education. On Sundays they would take me to Trenton, eleven miles away. I was enrolled in Sunday School at Temple *Adath Israel*. But for some reason, every Sunday I managed to be sick. Since I was hardly a sickly child, my parents soon got the message that I was miserable as an outsider and gave up on that part of my education.

Institutionalized religion always seemed strange and disappointing to me as a child. On the high holidays our family went to a little storefront *shul* on a side street in the business section of Princeton, N.J. To my knowledge, there were no daily or weekly services unless someone was observing a *yahrzeit*. The *shul* had a large front window that was covered with a roughly textured tan curtain. The floors and walls were institutionally bland and not very clean. In the back of the hall was a small altar and dais where the torah was kept and read. Behind that was the bathroom, which offered little privacy.

My uncles led the services, which were entirely in Hebrew with no English transliteration or translation and seemed interminable to me. Everyone sat on folding chairs – the men in front, the women behind them. The men were quite devout, wearing their prayer shawls and *yarmulkas*. The roomed buzzed with the sound of their voices as they *dovened*, swaying back and forth, intoning their prayers, each one going at his own speed. The women, who were less educated in Hebrew sat in back, leafing through their books and quietly talking among themselves. Everyone had a different prayer book. Of course, a few women like my grandmother and aunt were very pious. I remember my "*bubbe*", my grandmother, a tiny woman with a deeply lined face, who weighed about ninety pounds, standing on a folded white sheet in her cotton stocking feet, wearing her *shetle* or wig. I don't know why she took her shoes off to pray but I suppose the sheet was to keep her hose from getting dirty. She had an honored place in the first row of women and had a little stand to hold her books. I marveled that she could be so totally absorbed in her prayers that she was oblivious to the talking going on around her. Since my friends were not Jewish and went to beautiful churches, I was always embarrassed, worried that somehow my place for religion and perhaps my religion itself, did not measure up.

Just before my freshman year at college, my father arranged for us to go to High Holiday services at the beautiful, stately Temple *Ohabei Shalom* in Brookline. It was virtually the first time I had been with so many Jews in an established temple. Parts of the service were in English; other parts had translations of the Hebrew so that I could follow along. There also was beautiful music. Members of the congregation were warm and friendly. After services I remember commenting to my father that if we had belonged to such a temple it would have been easier to be Jewish in Princeton. Coincidentally, that was the temple where Bob's parents were members and the first temple we joined.

At any rate, while I was always questioning I never learned how to pray, except perhaps personal instinctual prayers of wishes or gratitude from my heart. Institutionalized prayers from prayer books and responsive reading have never resonated with me. Furthermore, I find that most of the English translations are in language that feels empty and archaic and is not mine. Our current prayer book does have interesting, well-written translations but this is quite new. What does help, however, are the prayers said or chanted in Hebrew where I don't need to know the meaning of the words. Just as in my childhood, these prayers are mantras that enable me to think, meditate, hope, reflect and be at peace. Perhaps there is a God or a supreme being who created our world with its natural rhythm and beauty. Certainly when I gave birth to a new child, a new living being, I felt each one was a glorious miracle. Was this new life a gift of God, our creator?

A friend who also lost a young son remarked that she repeatedly wrote in her journal about how enraged she was at God. I could understand how she felt but that was not my reaction or feeling. I don't think I believed enough in God to be angry. I just unhappily accepted our fate as part of being human.

I realize as I'm writing this that I have questioned religion and what I believe since I was young. Fortunately, in Reform Judaism you have the freedom to believe what you want. In my fifties I decided I had unfinished business and joined an adult Bat Mitzvah class. I enjoyed the intensive study, the discussions of philosophy, the self-examination and the introduction to Hebrew. At least I learned enough Hebrew so I can follow along and participate more easily in the service. But I have never developed a belief system like this anonymous quotation: "Faith sees the invisible, believes the incredible and receives the impossible." I wish I could believe this. My thinking is too concrete.

In my college chapel at the front of the altar were the words "God is Love". I can relate to that as a concept I can accept. In going through our own prayer book, I recently found a commentary by Mordecai Kaplan who said, "You shall love God intellectually, emotionally and with all your deeds. Whatever you love most in these ways is your god. For the Jewish people, the deepest love should be for freedom, justice and peace." Who can argue with that?

However, I find it hard to accept some of the formality and repetitions in our temple services or to have a personal faith that when we die we go to a better place. I think after you die, you are only your legacy and your legacy is what others remember about you. My mother died when she was forty-four and I was fourteen. I did not have enough time with her. However, I remember her voice and can still hear her precepts. "Remember the Golden Rule. A smile is the most contagious thing in the world. Always have a firm handshake. 'If' is a very big word. Don't promise anything you can't fulfill. Always try to find the best in people. Please and thank you are important words. Be modest about your accomplishments. Help people who are less fortunate than you. Always give money for charity."

Virtually everyone who knew my mother remembers her graciousness. They recall her gentleness, compassion, sense of fun and her social conscience. She was always ready to lend a hand or an ear. Most important was her music. She played the piano, sang and brought joy to those who heard her. That was part of her legacy. While my personality is much different, I have tried to pass on many of her values to my children. That's my understanding of our after life – i.e. what others remember about us.

I've often wondered how our sons will be remembered. Recently, I was reading some of the letters of condolence we received after the boys died. To my surprise, there were remarkably similar threads that ran through these notes that somehow described each boy's individuality and the impressions others had of them.

For example, almost everyone who knew Roger spoke of his striving to learn and to be like everyone else. They mentioned his amiability, his interest in talking about movies, books and other things that interested him and his grit. I came upon the notes Mark scribbled about his brother, which he said at the funeral.

> "Good bye Roger. You're dead now, but no one will forget you. Your specialness left its mark on everyone who knew you. You were a really nice person, kind and sincere and honest – qualities rare to find. Even when burdened like you were with unusual problems, you showed guts and a simple determination to be yourself. Maybe that's what we'll miss the most – your special presence, your uniquely alive character. We loved you, Rog, and we'll miss you a lot. You can be sure of that."

These tender words from his big brother actually captured Roger's spirit.

With Jon, people spoke of his intelligence and wit and how he loved to make people laugh. I remember sitting in our living room the night of his funeral. The room was full of Jonny's friends from high school and college.

"Do you remember when he put green paint on his face so that he would be an alien?"

"How about the time he was making faces at a boring speaker?"

"Do you remember the way he jazzed it up in the band?"

As they related their particular stories and anecdotes about him, we were all laughing as we recalled the smiles he brought to his friends as well as to us. I think this is what he would have wanted us to remember about him – his love of life and all it offered.

Of course, after Mark died there were many letters about the importance of his music but also about how he helped and encouraged other musicians. Throughout these words and at the funeral was the description of his passion to create, to be his own person, to march to the beat of whatever was driving him. No one said he was easy but he did make people think and laugh and through his music left a tangible memory.

These are the legacies of our sons. In my opinion, this is their afterlife.

So, if for me religion is mainly about one's deeds in life and leaving a legacy, why do I go to temple? It's because we wanted and needed the community and sense of belonging. In our Saturday *minyan* people warmly welcomed us. I like the music, chanting, study and the caring support. Although at this point we go to *minyan* fairly regularly on Saturday mornings, I join in but do not actually pray. During the Torah study that follows the lay led service I usually do not feel that I have much to offer, although I find the discussions interesting. I blame myself for this since most of my reading has been superficial and I have not given it the serious study that would make me have more to contribute.

Prior to our boys' deaths, I had not thought very much about the value of the ritual of sitting *shiva*. However, when each of them died it, became important to have the structure not only of customs but also rituals that have gone on for thousands of years. Since immediately after the funeral I did not want to face people or even to be part of the world, it actually was helpful to have to get up because I knew people would be coming to our house. I had to get dressed in order to accept our friends' sympathy. It was important to talk, to be with people, to feel their concern and desire to share our grief. It kept us, or at least me from retreating, which was what I wanted desperately to do. Each time, it seemed to me we found more solace from friends, family and tradition than we did, with a few exceptions, from our own clergy.

I think the let down was afterward when we were supposed to – had to – go on. At that time, I wondered if you could die of a broken heart. And sometimes I wanted to. That period was when we needed the support the most and when the community and even the familiarity of our temple and its rituals helped us. It was only by hearing from and being with people that we began to recover. We could not do it alone.

Recently I shared my thoughts and concerns with a classmate and long time friend, Dr. Letty M. Russell, a Presbyterian minister and professor *emerita* of Yale Divinity School. She was reassuring to me and thought perhaps I could formulate my beliefs in the following way:

I believe that human beings are created to:

Work for freedom, justice and peace in their world

Live in a community that cares for one another

And stretches over the ages

Remembering those whose love and life continues with us.

This statement was not only helpful to me, but also articulates what I believe.

What came next was the long, seemingly endless process of grieving, of dealing with the emptiness. In *A Potent Spell* [1], Janna Malamud Smith said, "To feel utterly bereft is unbearable," yet one has to bear the pain, to mourn the losses. I think it's fair to say that just as we loved each son differently, Bob, Martha and I each grieved for them differently.

[1] Janna Malamud Smith, *A Potent Spell: Mother Love and the Power of Fear*, Houghton Mifflin Company, Boston New York, 2003, (p.42).

DIFFERENT WAYS OF GRIEVING

---⚘---

WITH each son we grieved differently because we had different relationships with them. From my training as a social worker, I know that if you have had a conflicted relationship with someone who dies, the loss of that person becomes more complicated. It certainly was the case with Mark. While he had delighted us with his early development and successes, he also challenged us. He was always his own person and absolutely was not going to fit into any mold or more mundane life style and career that we might have had in mind for him. We tried to offer him possibilities; he preferred to make his choices from a different point of view and we were puzzled by what he chose.

He took much time and gave us a lot of angst. We had no idea what would become of him. Nevertheless, we tried to remain close and to accept him on his terms. Did we love him? Of course. He was our child. Did we like him? Sometimes, we did not. It was hard to be his parents. Did we let him know our values? Yes, and he let us know his. We often did not agree. He chose to be a rock musician; we were not in favor. We regret that we did not try harder to appreciate his music but we did not. If he had chosen to play classical, folk or even big band music, we could have understood him more easily. Our ears were not attuned to this new genre of music.

His death baffled us. Because I had worked on the head and neck service at Massachusetts Eye and Ear Infirmary where many of the patients had cancer, largely from smoking, I feared Mark, a heavy smoker, would get either lung or throat cancer or possibly end up with a laryngectomy. In fact, he already had polyps on his throat surgically removed. Thus, when he died of a massive heart attack, the cause of his death was totally unexpected.

At first, when we learned he died, we were numb – so numb we could hardly cry but were terribly sad. And I'm sure we were angry too.

145

There were so many unanswered questions. Why didn't Mark take better care of himself? Why did he smoke so much? Why did he burn the candle at both ends? Why was he so intense, not able to relax? Why did he have a heart attack? And we were also angry that he left so many loose ends for us to deal with. But most importantly we were angry that he was no longer with us when finally after his prolonged adolescence he had become a "*mensch*", a solid citizen.

By the time he died, we had finally learned to appreciate who he had become and his efforts to achieve his dreams. We liked his friends; we loved Sabine; we understood his aspirations. Then suddenly, he and his dreams were gone. I think of his out-of-the blue phone calls just to check in or to let us know he was about to take off on another trip or to tell us he was home safely. I miss his affection. I wonder what direction his life might have taken when he was supposed to return from his overseas performances. I miss reading about him and Morphine in the papers or staying up until way past midnight to see him on the Conan O'Brian Show when we could hardly stay awake. It was so hard to deal with all of his business affairs when all we wanted to do was mourn for our son. His financial obligations did not interest us at all and complicated our grief enormously. We wanted so much for him – success in his field yes, but we wanted him to be happy. We wanted him to be in our family. Part of our grieving for him was a yearning to keep our connections and to acknowledge how much was lost.

Fortunately Mark had a chance to realize himself. He knew who he was, what he wanted and what he might be able to achieve. Furthermore he died suddenly doing exactly what he wanted. His death was hard on the rest of us but perhaps a blessing for him to die as his musical career was soaring and his relationship with Sabine was defined.

As I said earlier, one way I deal with my feelings is to write. Thus, at the unveiling of his grave the following year, I wrote to him:

> "It still feels unfair that after all your hard work, your
> perseverance, your dedication to the purity of your art and
> the final acclaim that you earned and received that you
> could not live to enjoy it and to share your life with
> Sabine. You were a reader, thinker, writer, philosopher –
> you were a late bloomer but you really blossomed and did
> it all your way. You lived to develop your dream – your

music the way you heard it and with people who shared your vision. You developed a style, you wrote your feelings, you made people laugh. Now at your final resting place, we mourn for the loss of your spirit, your humor, your hugs, your warmth, your love. Still, you left a legacy – a whole gamut of memories – some sweet, some painful. It's those memories we'll hold onto and cherish."

* * *

There were fewer complications with the other boys. With Roger we saw what was going on. Even in seven weeks there was a period of anticipatory grief. We knew it was coming. A few friends or family called us at the hospital and I said tearfully, "Roger is dying." Inevitably their response was, "Oh, no. He'll get better. He's in a fine hospital with excellent doctors. He'll recover." But we knew he would not. Nothing was going well. He had one middle-of-the-night crisis after the other. With each operation we knew Roger's condition was getting worse and therefore we had time to process it all. While we tried to be positive and hopeful, we knew in our hearts his prognosis was grim. Somehow facing a medical situation and dealing with a medical staff that was mainly supportive, we came to accept the inevitable. By the time he died, we knew everything possible had been done for him and that Roger was doomed.

Roger was more dependent on us than the others. We had done the best we could for him but his whole life had been a struggle. While we had hoped he would find his way in the world, we knew he would have continued to face many obstacles and his life would not have been easy. None of this made us love him or miss him less but probably for these reasons his death was more understandable to us and more acceptable than Jonny's accident and Mark's totally unexpected heart attack.

Jon's death made no sense to us at all. There was no process involved. There was neither rhyme nor reason for him to fall out of a window on a cold February night and die. He had been a sensible kid. His fall was totally unlike him. He was with people we did not know and we have always been haunted by his unnecessary, inexplicable death. We felt that his death was somehow tainted, that there was something dirty or clouded about it. Jonny was healthy, promising and just beginning to enter the adult world and suddenly his life was over. It was absolutely unacceptable then, still is, and probably always will be.

At the unveiling of his marker, I wrote the following about him.

"It's hard to believe it was such a short time ago that Jon was with us to unveil his younger brother's marker. Now just a year and a half later our smaller family gathers again. Jonny was only beginning to venture into the world – to try on different hats to see where he was comfortable, who he was. This is the time to remember his blithe, breezy manner, his funny sense of humor, his grins, his playfulness, his spirit of adventure, his enjoyment of people, his thoughtfulness and even his wisdom. He liked to make people laugh, whether through jazzing on his saxophone, weaving ridiculous stories, dressing in silly costumes or making grimaces – people enjoyed him. In fact, he always had a lot of good, loyal friends. There wasn't much about him not to like.

He was quite human – not perfect. There were the usual adolescent struggles – testing – some painful acting out. But how we miss him and his grin, his hugs, his sunshine that he brought to all who knew him! We ache when we think of him, yet must now go on and hold onto our memories and feel glad that we had him for as long as we did. Our loving goes on."

With the younger boys everything was clean. Their financial affairs were simple and straightforward. We were in charge; we made the decisions about memorial funds. They had no assets to speak of so we had to deal with funerals and grief and loneliness and anger and despair but not money and lawyers. Also, we did not have all the business pressures and complicated relationships; we did not have to deal with the publicity and all the people we did not know. Our relationships with the younger boys were clearer. They had not challenged us the way Mark had. They were easier and more compliant, so in a crazy way their deaths were less complicated too.

The fact that there was so much publicity around Mark's death made us feel that the other boys were shortchanged. There was nothing in the media about them; there were no recordings. We can continue to listen to Mark's voice and his music, but it's hard to hear his voice and know that he's no longer here and never will be. We can only hear the younger boys in our heads. What kind of legacy did Jon and Roger leave except what's in our hearts? Nothing tangible. Does that mean their lives were worth less? Not to us. They never had the chance to affect the world as Mark did. They were too young, too young.

I have regrets about Jonny and Roger. I wonder what they would have chosen for careers, for mates, for their life styles. We'll never know. That they did not even have a chance hurts us always. For each of our boys, we can only ask, why? Why? Why did this awfulness happen? Yet we know there are no answers and we have to go on the best we can. We have to make a life for ourselves. We need to find things to look forward to, even as we age. We need to hold on to the good memories and to forgive ourselves for our mistakes. But I feel we'll always be damaged and see ourselves as different from other people who, though they might have had problems with their kids, have children who are still alive. We'll always long to have our whole family back.

I feel so sad now to have only one child out of four. I was an only child – a lonely kid who longed for a brother or sister and wanted to have a big lively family. That was my dream and I thought Bob and I had created one. And now Martha was left alone. Yes, she had had her differences with her brothers. They squabbled and teased and annoyed each other. But they were connected. They were a family. Martha was a wonderful, thoughtful sister to Roger who needed her. She was a buddy to Jon – the two in the middle who probably profited from healthy neglect as their parents had to put so much energy into the other two.

It took a long time but Martha and Mark had finally become friends. I think Sabine helped because Martha really liked her. It made us glad to know she invited Mark and Sabine to her home without us. Martha appreciated Mark's music in a way that Bob and I did not and while she was unable to attend most of his performances she invited him to come to her classes to talk about how his music was made. It made both of them feel good and close.

After Mark died and Martha was left as the one survivor, I felt dreadful for her and knew that Mark's death was frightening and devastating to her. Fortunately someone pointed out that Martha is not an only child; she had a history of having had three brothers. But at least she had that experience. I remember after Mark's funeral when we were on the way to the cemetery, Martha commented sadly that she had learned from her friend Christy to say in Norwegian, "I have three brothers." And now she had none. It was tragic. I had wished for siblings and didn't have them. It's much harder, I think, to have brothers and lose them.

Martha rarely talked about her feelings yet she had to have been deeply affected by losing her brothers. Although she kept her emotions to herself, she grieved in her own way. She did not seem to need to talk as much as I did. In fact she and I rarely talk together about our grief. At the unveiling of Mark's marker in the cemetery, Bob and I had written what we wanted to say but thought Martha might want to read something from the liturgy about sibling loss. Unfortunately, we had not shown this to her ahead of time. However, Martha started to read in the stilted language of the prayer book:

> "...I have come to this sacred place where rests my dear brother with whom I grew up, sharing the play of childhood... Death parted us too soon. There is no limit to my grief, when I think that we, whom one mother nourished and sheltered, are forever separated..."

And then she sobbed. This was too much for her; she clearly was hurting.

When everyone feels so raw, what happens to family relationships? How do we share the pain? It's not easy. There's no magic way to deal with loss. We each indulge our own feelings and have to work through them, to process what we experienced, to feel sad and then move on. I feel very close to Martha and freely express my emotions – happy or sad. We talk about day-to-day events and what's going on with her and her children; we share many meals; we enjoy going to all of her, her children's and her students' musical performances. She includes us as much as she can but prefers to be independent and have her privacy. She is not a worrier or at least doesn't talk about her concerns with us. "You worry enough for the whole family, Mom. The rest of us don't have to worry!" On the other hand, I feel that she tries to shield us from things that are not going well or that might disturb us. I would rather know the whole story but need to respect what she wants to share.

Of course, not only our family was grieving. Each of the boys had friends who were disturbed and probably frightened by the death of a contemporary. Young people feel immortal, but when they experience the loss of someone their own age, it is threatening and sobering. For us, it is bittersweet when their friends greet us warmly. Most of Jonny's friends turned fifty this year so there was a round of big birthday celebrations. This made us acutely aware of the passage of time since we think of him and them as twenty-three. And we wonder what Jon's life would have been like? How would he have celebrated?

After Mark died, his close friends grieved in their own way. They started the Mark Sandman Music Education Fund which has given many young people the opportunities to learn and appreciate creative music. His friends, especially Sabine, Billy Conway, Dana Colley and Deb Klein, organized two benefit concerts at the corner of Massachusetts and Brookline Avenues where the Middle East Restaurant is. At those events, Billy, Dana and other musicians played primarily Mark's music to raise money for the fund. Both performances were highly successful. Also, at that corner, a new street sign was installed and designated Mark Sandman Square. It is a fitting tribute in a most appropriate space.

Soon after Mark died, his many musician friends gathered together to form Orchestra Morphine which gave the music a bigger, more exotic sound. The group traveled around this country and Europe. In addition, they gave a big concert at the Somerville Theater, which we attended. They played Mark's music as a way to remember him and to deal with their own grief. After all, they not only lost their friends, but also the life they had known. We hope these efforts helped to assuage their grief and enabled them to find new directions for themselves.

The townspeople of Palestrina had a memorial for Mark a year after he died. Many of his friends went; the mayor of the town spoke; a large bouquet of sunflowers was given to Sabine; and a bronze memorial plaque was installed on the stairway to the park. Although we chose not to go at that time, we went by ourselves a few months later for our own private memorial as we went to see where he had died. I'm sure it was therapeutic for us, and I assume for Mark's friends, to be there.

So we all deal with our feelings in our own way. For Bob and me it has been hard to have tried to build a big, close family and now to have a small more intimate one. Do these shared tragedies bring us closer than we might have been? Who knows? It just means all of us are hurting. And what lies ahead? How do we go on?

Bob and I: Where We Are Now

"How do you go on?" This is the question we hear the most. And we wonder. What choices do we have? We could either retreat from life or try to look ahead, appreciate what we have and invest in the future. Are our lives colored by our tragedies? Of course. Do we look at our future with the same optimism we once had? No. Our hearts are broken but still we struggle to be productive and to keep our friends without drowning them in our grief. We can't talk about it but we long to be rid of our broken hearts.

Do we talk about the boys? Yes, but judiciously. Most people, especially strangers, don't want to hear our story. It's too threatening. I'll mention in general conversation that one of our boys did something in school or on their travels. That's part of ordinary, social dialogue. If the next question or comment is what is he doing now? Then I'll answer candidly that he is no longer living. Usually the person will apologize or say he's sorry and the conversation will go elsewhere. Sometimes the person will probe more. I try to respond openly and only give direct answers to their queries. Rarely do I say, well that son died but so did our two other sons. That's much too heavy for someone who has no history with us.

At one time, we were at a party where we only knew one other couple. As the conversation turned to getting acquainted, people spoke about their children. At times like these, I tend to shrink back and become quiet. I'm interested in other people's families but don't particularly want to talk about ours. When the inevitable questions, "Do you have children?" or "How many children do you have?" came up, I said we have a daughter and grandchildren in Newton. It did not seem to be the time or place to say more. However, what I really wanted to say was, "We are fortunate to have a lovely daughter and three wonderful grandchildren but we have tragically lost our three sons." It's always a hard one to call.

I also don't like it when people recite from Ecclesiastes, "To everything there is a season." I know this is true for a time to plant, a time to reap, and a time of war, a time of peace. It's also true for a time to laugh, a time to weep, a time to be born, a time to die. It's the last that bothers me, because I felt each of our sons died before his time. For every one it certainly was too early. The hardest part of losing children is that it's the wrong order of life events. I think most parents who have sat with a dying child or have even been with a critically ill child wishes he or she could take the child's place. I know we felt that way, but no one has that option.

In a novel by Julius Lester, one of the characters who had lost her son in Viet Nam asked, "How do you bury the child you birthed? How do you watch the children of your neighbors getting their first jobs, marrying and bringing grandchildren for visits on Sunday afternoons and you have only memories you don't know how to hold?"[1] These issues come up for us when we see the families of our friends. We longingly watch their children, our children's friends, mature, develop careers, get married and have their own children. And we take pleasure in this – but we also feel that a big part of our lives is missing.

These, too, were some of the questions that occurred to me when I saw Jonny in my vision. Our boys' lives were not finished; in fact for two of them, their adult lives were just beginning. But just as each of them lost his future so did we lose ours. We lost our hopes and dreams for our sons, for a large family, for us in our old age.

We have had some strange encounters. We were at a lecture to hear a visiting speaker who, in the course of his talk, had mentioned he lost a child. Afterward one of our friends suggested we meet him since we had that experience in common. We were introduced and I said, "Although our circumstances were different we can understand what you've been through because we have lost three sons and it is so very hard and sad." The speaker, who was quite renowned and an expert on grief, said, "I could survive one child's death but not another," at which point he turned on his heels and walked away. Bob and I were left feeling exposed and tarnished.

Sometimes it feels as if our bad luck might be contagious. If people know us and have a history with us, it is easier. We have shared memories and can speak more freely. If our friends and family find us diffi-

---

[1] Julius Lester, *The Autobiography of God*, St. Martin's Press, New York, 2004, (p.63).

cult to be with, that's too bad. It's the way it is. But when people don't know us it's always more difficult. If we talk, it's a show stopper; if we don't, it feels like we're hiding something. I often sense that we have become labeled as the couple that has lost their three sons. I feel that these losses have become an integral part of our identities.

Right after each of the boys died, I wanted to, needed to talk, to tell their story, to let people know how awful we felt – I felt. Sometimes I could feel friends back away from me as my talking got out of control; other times I was aware that they were uncomfortable. Most of the time I tried to read the cues and stop talking. The last thing we wanted was to make others uneasy around us. When the losses were very new and we entered a group where we were known, I could perceive the tension as some friends either had the courage to come over and say they were sorry or others who were too uncomfortable to say anything. Therefore the interchanges that were usually easy became strained. All we wanted was for people to say, "I'm sorry." There's not much else to say.

It's hard to explain how Bob and I have maintained our marriage through these deaths. While we clung to each other, I can understand why so many marriages fail after losing a child at any age. Children are a product of your love; they are an intrinsic part of your lives; they are people you have cherished and worried over and been proud of and reared together. When they are gone the hole is so deep and you feel so empty, you really have nothing to give to each other. Shared memories bring deep sadness as you recall both the good times and the struggles. Life will never be the same. The phone calls, the letters, the hugs will never be there so you have to shift gears and make a new path. For some, continuing on in the old way is just too painful.

For us too, it hasn't been easy. I think when we married we made promises to each other that we'd stick it out together through thick and thin. Those were real commitments that have become the frame-work through which we operate. As Madeleine L'Engle wrote in *A Circle of Quiet*, the first in a trilogy of her memoirs about her family, "We would never have reached the relationship we have today if we hadn't made promises. Perhaps we made them youthfully and blindly, not knowing all that was implied, but the very promises have been a saving grace"[2].

[2]Madeleine L'Engle, *A Circle of Quiet*, Harper, San Francisco, CA, 1972, (p.107).

It's not only our commitment to each other that has preserved our marriage but also a bit of good luck. As Judith Viorst wrote about her own marital relationship, "We've learned over time, ways of working with the imperfections inherent in being married…"[3] and so did we.

Early in our marriage we had defined our respective roles which have changed somewhat over the years, but which have given us a *modus vivendi* that has worked. Judith Viorst also said that marriage takes "patience, perseverance, sacrifice and generosity,"[4] For us, it also takes a lot of compromising

Bob was the chief breadwinner and a loving father, but he was not home very much. He enjoyed his business and professional work and was a workaholic, which I believe he now regrets. He was active in local politics, chaired committees, and cared deeply about his community. All of this activity was basic to his personality and still is. Whatever he does, he pours his heart into and does thoroughly. He certainly was our major source of income and was a steady provider.

Whenever I worked, and surely after I began my professional career, mine was to be a second income for saving or for fun. It didn't always work that way since we have had several major financial upheavals when Bob was glad to have what I had saved to bail us out. My big job was to manage the children and household. Even when I returned to graduate school, my responsibilities at home continued; there were always meals on the table and clean socks in everyone's drawer. I would continue to arrange the childcare, car pools and a social life for us. Because Bob worked extraordinarily long days he was much less involved with the children than I. Therefore I blamed myself when things went wrong. If they were my responsibility, it must have been my fault that Mark was acting out or Roger had learning difficulties. "Trouble with children at any age can make for trouble between a husband and wife."[5] And we were no exception. However, in retrospect I could have asked Bob for more help or he could have offered but it did not happen.

---

[3]Judith Viorst, *Grown-Up Marriage*, The Free Press, A Civision of Simon and Shuster, Inc., New York, NY, 2003, (p. 233).

[4]Ibid. (p. 262).

[5]Ibid. (p. 224).

Bob loves to entertain, and so do I. While we lived in our big house in Waban, we had lots of parties – dinner for friends, political gatherings, parties to mark special occasions such as birthdays and anniversaries. I miss this aspect of our lives. Now there seem to be fewer occasions to celebrate and our new home does not lend itself to big gatherings. Furthermore, most of our friends seem to be spending more time with their growing families and their many activities and events. When you have a large family, the natural progression is for the children to have their own families so there are more and more events to attend and savor. We, too, had anticipated a growing family, but now often feel lonely at holidays and are sensitive to the many empty chairs at our celebrations. We are painfully aware that our circle of family and friends has become more limited.

Bob and I talk very little together about our losses. Often, when we return home after being with other families, we comment about how we long to have our big family too. It is a dashed dream that the family we had thought would be large is now so small. Mainly the two of us just slog along and try to cope with each day. I don't think it ever occurred to us to go separate ways. Perhaps the old Yiddish expression, "old love doesn't rust," applies to us and there is a basic trust in each other.

As of now, we have a lot of togetherness. This works as long as we each have our own physical and emotional space. I feel fortunate that even when we downsized, Bob has a room for his office in the basement and I have my own computer in my office up-stairs. I feel this is crucial for our sanity, or at least for mine. I really need privacy and a place to be alone.

I don't mean to imply that we never argue or get angry at each other. We used to spend endless hours discussing the children's problems and what to do about them. Presently, our arguments are more mundane. We differ about money issues. I am much more conservative than he. We squabble about, "Where did I leave my keys? Or my eyeglasses? Or my papers?" We accuse each other of being forgetful or inattentive or hard of hearing. I am compulsively prompt and get impatient if I have to wait; Bob rarely worries about time and tends to do things at the last minute. If he's a little late, that's OK with him but not with me. Still, basically we understand each other and get along. And finally and most importantly, we always like to get into bed at night and find comfort and security in our physical closeness.

157

When one era ends, another begins. For us the next era was literally entering a new and probably final stage of our own lives. When Mark died, Bob was already retired and I was still working part-time. We had just moved from our family home and neighborhood. But we really did not know what had hit us. Bob was working on Mark's financial and legal affairs. The business aspects of dealing with Mark's estate have impeded the grief process for us and certainly prolonged it. The public outpouring of tributes and sadness was gratifying but made it harder to cope with the business aspects of his public life and our very personal grief. We're still working on this. Meanwhile I tried to deal with everyone's feelings.

I think sibling loss does not get enough attention. People seem to be more concerned about parents than other children in the family. But when you grow up with the same parents in the same household you share a lot. Of course there is jealousy and competition and resentment; but there is also a strong bond and love.

I don't know how Martha managed but she seemed to have her priorities straight. She had her young family, her husband, her profession to deal with and she had us. She did not sink, nor wallow in self-pity, nor outwardly dwell on her own sadness. She was much like Bob. You have to rise to the circumstances and cope with the emotions later. This, at least, was my observation. She certainly did not crumble, nor did she talk to us about her concerns or grief.

Now we are overwhelmed with her many successes. She has blossomed into an extremely competent, self-assured woman who continues to be a leader in her field and takes on increasing responsibilities in organizing conferences for the Organization of American Kodaly Educators and conducting and participating in choral groups. We are dazzled by her growth and abilities. We are also grateful that she invites us to attend her students' performances. When we go to her school and listen to the earnest but ragged orchestra and band concerts of nine and ten year olds who have only been playing their instruments for a few months or year, we have to chuckle. It brings back so many memories.

Over the years, Ted has grown into our family and seems more comfortable. He has now found a balance in his life – his profession, his running marathons and his involvement with family, friends and the Unitarian Church. Even though he works hard and often at odd hours, he manages to be at important events for Martha and the children. Of course, he always has projects in their house. Sometimes it's plumbing or electrical work or replacing windows but he likes to make things work properly. We are proud of him and glad he's part of our family.

Watching our grandchildren mature and become interesting people has been a treat for us. The boys, Alex and Gabe, graduated from Colgate and Skidmore respectively and have begun jobs in their fields of business and economics. They wanted some work experience before they go on to graduate school. Amanda has become a beautiful high school girl who is interested at present in science, music and languages. We love sharing events with them and going to their athletic and musical performances.

Our involvement with Martha's family is what makes our lives bearable. It's an arduous road. People ask what has helped us. For me, my professional training has been minimally helpful. I have worked with others who have had devastating losses, have listened to their sorrows, have offered sympathy and consolation and encouraged them to tell their stories over and over again. When our sons died, I needed the same. I was fortunate to work in hospitals, where my colleagues were accustomed to life threatening illness and death, and perhaps instinctively they reached out to me and encouraged me to talk. I doubt that my actual training was useful. When death happens to someone in your own family, it is so acutely personal and irrational that your training is of little value. You are just another victim or survivor. Nevertheless, I did get a great deal of support. It was a caring environment. I was also fortunate to have close friends who patiently listened and stood by me. I know Bob did not have that advantage and I don't think Martha did either.

Professional training does not help a lot when you are confronted with a personal tragedy but it helps somewhat to know that your irrational feelings and experiences, like seeing a lost one when he is not there, couldn't be there, are normal. Groups such as *Compassionate Friends*, a nation wide organization for parents who have lost children, are helpful for some. When Bob and I attended a meeting after Jonny died, we did not find it useful at all. Groups are good for some but this was not for us.

We each had to find ways to ease our pain. For me, having a few close friends, being able to tell our story and to write about our experience has been therapeutic. Over the years I have seen a number of psychotherapists and they have been helpful to me. Mainly they listened to my story over and over again. They were kind and patient and I needed them. Otherwise I would have worn out our friendships. For a while anti-depressants were prescribed for me. They lightened my mood somewhat.

Very important to me has been and is, physical activity – either at a gym or simply by walking. I found that building an exercise program into my daily life makes me feel better and in more control of my life. Perhaps I spend too much time and money taking care of myself but I know that if I don't I will not be functional. Bob and Martha have had to find their own path; their style is different from mine and they seek less outside help.

After the boys died, I felt compelled to read anything that had to do with death. I have gone to many conferences and workshops on death, grief and bereavement. Reading suggested ways of coping does not seem to work for me. I was not interested in "self-help" books or formulas on how to cope. What was useful to me were personal stories, memoirs of others' experiences with loss and how they survived or didn't. Who was affected? How did they manage? Did they fall apart or retreat? Even sitting in the hospital waiting room while Roger was dying, I remember reading Gerda Lerner's *A Death of One's Own*. It was not cheerful reading but something to which I could relate and appreciate what the author was feeling. When I read novels, I seem drawn to situations where people, especially children, have died and it is helpful to me to learn the emotions and coping mechanisms characters had.

With the loss of a child, or two or three, you never "get over it" nor are completely healed. It feels like there is a scab covering a wound that can easily be reopened. I believe there's always a layer of sadness shadowing our lives and probably Martha's too, although sibling loss is different. I do not believe this is pathological. In Jewish tradition, as I understand it, there is a period of *shiva* for one week, another period of a month of *schloshim,* a year of saying *yahrzeit* and then you go on with your life. In my opinion, that does not apply to child loss. What I learned from Dr. Hunter was that when you write, you concretize the experience. Putting together a narrative of our family has been necessary, affirming, therapeutic and certainly cathartic. It has given me more energy, a greater sense of peace and optimism for the future. When the story is written, it's more tangible and you can deal with it better. However, the pain and longing to have your children back never goes away and I don't think ever will.

Now that we are in our seventies, what do we look forward to? We still like to be with friends; we enjoy traveling of all kinds, whether a rubber tubing expedition in Belize, a cruise through the Panama Canal or around Cape Horn or renting a house with friends in Mexico. We go to theater, concerts, and lectures. We take courses to try to keep our minds active. We want to be needed and to be helpful to others. We enjoy being with our friends and family. But perhaps most important, we like to be with each other.

We think we will never get over our losses and probably don't want to. Each day we long for our children and irrationally hope they'll return. We want and need to validate our sons' lives. We'll always love them. While we go on, they remain static. We need to keep involved, to have new experiences, to learn, to grow, to have some adventures and to be useful to others. We need to laugh and invest in the future, to be part of life. Leonard Fein said that living when you have lost a child is like living with "the enduring presence of an absence[6]." We feel that times three.

[6] Leonard Fein, *Against the Dying of the Light*, Jewish Lights Publishing, Woodstock, Vermont, 2001, (p.105).

AFTERWARD

We remember the ones we have loved who are no longer with us. We love them; we think of them, we remember them. There are tears in our remembering; and there are smiles as well.

We give thanks; remembering is a gift.
We give thanks; their lives are a blessing.
We give thanks for what we had.
We give thanks for what we have.

We remember the good as though it were yesterday.
And the bad has been softened by the passing seasons.
Good and bad alike, laughter and tears alike, are ours.
Remembering is a gift,
a gift of love passing back and forth
among yesterdays,
among those that were and those that are,
those we walk with now, and those with whom we walked but yesterday
for whose journey we are glad.[1]

IN LOVING MEMORY OF:

ROGER ELIOT SANDMAN

JONATHAN MAYNARD SANDMAN

MARK JEFFREY SANDMAN

---

[1] *Shaarei Simchah–Gates of Joy*, an independently published prayerbook for the festivals, by Rabbi Chaim Stern.

Tel and Bob 2002

ACKNOWLEDGEMENTS

I wish to thank many who were not mentioned by name in this book but who were very helpful to us. Our cousins Drs. Ralph Bransky, Joseph Solovy and Lawrence Cohen gave us much advice during Roger's illness and helped us know what questions to ask. Dr. William Norwood, Roger's cardiac surgeon, responded to repeated crises no matter the time day or night and was always helpful, available and sympathetic.

Without the help and encouragement from Dr. Allan Hunter, my writing coach, Miriam Goodman, my editor and Nancy Patton, my copy editor this would not have been written.

I am indebted to Anne Levin who read several versions of this work, made corrections and offered gentle criticism. My gratitude goes to Janet Polansky, Dorothy Irving and Karen Davis (my writing group), who patiently listened and offered constructive criticism to version after version. To my many friends and colleagues who read the book or parts of it, especially Ro Griesse, Molly Jane Isaacson Rubinger, Janet Sprague, Margaret Carlson and Pat Endy I am most grateful. Sabine Hrechdakian read the chapters on Mark and offered suggestions, contributions and important corrections. This was a special gift to me.

Most importantly, I thank Martha, our daughter, who clarified many points, read copy and listened to and understood my struggles and to her husband, Ted Holmes, who rescued me from my technological frustrations.

My primary helper and patient reader was Bob, who shared this journey with me, who read copy after copy and who encouraged me every step of the way. It is his story too.

Guitelle Sandman, LICSW, is a retired social worker. She was educated at Wellesley College and at Simmons College School of Social Work. For many years she worked at Boston Hospital for Women, at Brigham and Women's Hospital and at Massachusetts Eye and Ear Infirmary, as well as in private practice, where her specialties were in oncology and sensory loss. She published articles and presented papers at professional conferences. Throughout her career, she was a working mother with a strong commitment to and focus on her family. She currently lives in Waltham, MA.

63380963R00102

Made in the USA
Charleston, SC
03 November 2016